KEEPING
YOU
A SECRET

A NOVEL BY
JULIE ANNE PETERS

Megan Tingley Books
LITTLE, BROWN AND COMPANY
New York   Boston

ALSO BY JULIE ANNE PETERS:

Between Mom and Jo
Define "Normal"
grl2grl
Luna
Pretend You Love Me
She Loves You, She Loves You Not . . .

Little, Brown and Company

Hachette Book Group
237 Park Avenue, New York, NY 10017
Visit our website at www.lb-teens.com

Little, Brown and Company is a division of Hachette Book Group, Inc.
The Little, Brown name and logo are trademarks of Hachette Book Group, Inc.

The publisher is not responsible for websites (or their content) that are not owned by the publisher.

First Paperback Edition: May 2005
First published in hardcover in May 2003 by Little, Brown and Company

The characters and events portrayed in this book are fictitious. Any similarity to real persons, living or dead, is coincidental and not intended by the author.

Library of Congress Cataloging-in-Publication Data

Peters, Julie Anne.
Keeping you a secret / by Julie Anne Peters.—1st ed.
p. cm.
Summary: As she begins a very tough last semester of high school, Holland finds herself puzzled about her future and intrigued by a transfer student who wants to start a Lesbigay club at school.
ISBN 978-0-316-70275-1 (hc) / ISBN 978-0-316-00985-0 (pb)
[1. Interpersonal relations—Fiction. 2. Lesbians—Fiction. 3. High schools—Fiction 4. Schools—Fiction.
5. Stepfamilies—Fiction. 6. College choice—Fiction.] 1. Title.
PZ7.P44158 Ke 2003
[Fic]—dc21

10 9 8 7
RRD-C

Printed in the United States of America

To Sherri
for always

▼▲▼

And to those who are living out and proud.
You are a beacon for others to find their way home.

KEEPING
YOU
A SECRET

Chapter 1

*F*irst time I saw her was in the mirror on my locker door. I'd kicked my swim gear onto the bottom shelf and was reaching to the top for my calc book when she opened her locker across the hall. She had a streaked blond ponytail dangling out the back of her baseball cap.

Great. Now I was obligated to rag on her for violating the new dress code. Forget it, I decided. My vote — the only dissenting one in the whole student council — still counted. With me, anyway. People could come to school buck naked for all I cared. It wasn't about clothes.

We slammed our lockers in unison and turned. Her eyes met mine. "Hi," she said, smiling.

My stomach fluttered. "Hi," I answered automatically. She was new. Had to be. I would've noticed her.

She sauntered away, but not before I caught a glimpse of her T-shirt. It said: IMRU?

Am I *what?*

She glanced back over her shoulder, the way you do when you

know someone's watching. That's when it registered — the rainbow triangle below the message. My eyes dropped. Kept her in sight, though, as she disappeared around the corner.

I shifted my attention to my schedule. Brit Lit, calc, U.S. History, then art and econ after lunch. Was I out of my mind? Why was I taking a full load my last semester of high school? Weren't we supposed to revel in this time, embrace our friends, screw around until graduation? At some pivotal point, of course, we'd decide the direction our lives were going to take. A derisive laugh might've escaped my lips. Like I got to decide anything about my life.

I headed down the deserted hallway, clutching my books to my chest. This is insane, I thought. I don't even need the credits. I'd gotten to choose the early track — first class at seven, last class at one — but then I added econ at the last minute so I'd be finishing the day with everyone else. I drew a deep breath — and coughed. Who needed to get stoned before school when you got a free ride from the carpet-cleaning fumes?

Morning was a blur. As I stumbled to lunch, my head reeling from the volume of homework I'd already accumulated, my anxiety mounted. I'd be up till midnight, easy.

"Babe!" Seth called across the crowded cafeteria. He loped to the double doorway to meet me. Kiss me. "We're over here." He thumbed toward the vending machines, snaking an arm around my waist and steering me along.

"Hi, Holland. Hey, Seth," a few people greeted us as we weaved between tables. I assumed my oh-so-happy face. Plaster-casted smile. What was wrong with me? I loved school. I couldn't wait to get back after winter break.

2

"Holland, did you see Mrs. Lucas? She was looking for you," Leah said as she cleared a place beside her for me to sit. "She said to tell you to drop into the career center sometime today."

Today, tomorrow, never. Popping the top on a can of Pepsi Twist that Seth had set in front of me, I said to Kirsten across the table, "How was Christmas in Texas?"

Leah kicked my shin.

Uh-oh.

Kirsten sighed theatrically. "You had to ask." She launched into a psychodrama about how her mother was a raving lunatic the whole two weeks and all they did was scream at each other.

Seth split his fries with me and I zoned. He said in my ear, "You want ketchup?" I must've nodded because he got up and left.

Leah and Kirsten began to talk about college — again. Could we get through one whole day without bringing up the subject? Kirsten said, "Mom wants me to commute to Metro Urban and live at home. Like *that's* going to happen." She rolled her eyes. "All I want to do is graduate and get the hell out of this rat hole."

I checked out again. At some point Seth returned with the ketchup and I swabbed a greasy fry through the watery blob. Round and round it goes; where it stops, nobody knows. Seth nudged me. "You okay?"

I glanced up to find everyone staring at me. Was I chanting out loud? Relinquishing my hold on the mutilated fry, I crossed my eyes and said, "I got Arbuthnot for Brit Lit."

They all went, "Eeooh." Leah added, "Don't ever be late. She'll ream you out in front of everyone."

I grimaced. I hated when teachers did that. "You know," I said, picking up my cheeseburger, "all these anti-bullying policies should apply to teachers. I mean, *corporal* punishment is illegal." I chomped into my burger and chewed. "Public humiliation," I said with my mouth full, "is a form of *psychological* abuse."

By their bobbing heads, I assumed they all agreed. What were we going to do about it? Nothing. Even though I was president of student council, I felt powerless to effect change of any social significance at our school.

I take that back. We now had a pop machine in the hall.

▼▲▼

Drawing Level I was, as Seth referred to it, a bullshit class. But I needed to fill time between lunch and econ. As I wandered down the arts wing, feeling totally out of my element, I wondered what mental aberration had possessed me when I chose an art elective. Drawing, no less, which probably required talent. More than doodling in notebooks.

The assigned studio, 212A, had four rows of tables set end-to-end with chairs arranged haphazardly. No semblance of order. I slid into a plasti-seat in the back. My uneasiness grew as I studied the crowd clogging the doorway and milling around the display cases. Not the kind of people I usually associated with — which was okay. I didn't have a problem with diversity. It was just . . . I don't know. I felt weird. I decided to drop the class. Maybe add another study hall. I was going to need it.

A man's voice in the hallway herded everyone inside. As people filed across the threshold, I caught sight of her. The baseball cap was gone; now her hair flowed around her shoulders.

Her eyes darted across the studio and stopped on me. I wanted to look away, but couldn't. She held me somehow, spellbound.

The instructor bustled in and broke the connection. Oh, God. He looked like Einstein on ecstasy. "Just find a seat anywhere," he said to the stragglers. As he turned to write his name on the board, I flipped open a spiral. When I glanced over surreptitiously, she'd slipped into a seat up front. Another girl slid in beside her. I knew that girl — Randi or Brandi. She was on swim team last year for about a week. Right about the time Seth and I hooked up. Brandi.

"I realize you can't read this," the instructor said as he ran a palm over his cotton candy hair, "but it says 'Jonathan McElwain.'" He was right. His handwriting was gorgeous, all loopy and bold, but you'd need clearer vision than mine to decipher it. I squinted through my contacts — that was an *M?* He brushed chalk off his hands and added, "You can call me Mackel."

I wrote down, *Mr. McElwain.* Then drew a line through it and printed, *Mackel.*

"If I want to get paid, I have to turn this in." He flapped a computer printout at us. Hopping onto the desk, he curled crosslegged and uncapped a Flair. "Anderson, Michaela."

"Present." A girl at the end of my row raised her hand, and Mackel scratched a checkmark.

A few people I did actually know. It's inevitable when you've lived in the same place your whole life. The guy with the serious orange spikes and nostril ring was in my calc class. Winslow Demming. I remembered him from computer science sophomore year, except back then Winslow was a geek. Brilliant, though. And sweet. Another reminder why people shouldn't be judged on appearance.

Mr. McElwain — Mackel — progressed through the list. For some reason I was focusing on the back of the blond girl's head, only half listening for my name. "Cecelia Goddard," Mackel read. Her hand shot up and she said, "It's Cece."

I wrote it down. *Cecelia Goddard. CC? Cece?*

Cece, I decided and drew a box around it.

"Holland Jaeger."

A couple of heads swiveled. "What?" I blinked up.

"Holland Jaeger?"

"Oh, here." I raised my hand. Added in a mutter, "Apparently not *all* here."

She twisted around and smiled. My stomach lurched. I shielded my face with my hand and pretended to scribble notes.

Mackel handed out a supplies list. It was long. There were pencils, ink, charcoal, erasers, markers, pens, two sizes of drawing tablets. God, I'd have to work a month of overtime to afford all this stuff. Mackel said, "I know it's a short week, but I'd appreciate it if you could get your supplies in the next couple of days. Go to Hobby Lobby or Wal-Mart for the best prices. If anyone has real financial need, come see me after class. That doesn't mean you'd rather spend your money on a kegger." He eagle-eyed the room. "But I have a starving artist fund, so don't be shy."

I liked that. He was understanding. Maybe I'd wait to drop.

▼▲▼

At two-fifteen the bell rang and I gathered my books and notes from econ, feeling totally brain-dead. Lockers banged open and closed as I trudged down the hall. "Hi, Holland. Have a good break?" someone called.

"Great, thanks." I waved, plastering on The Smile. Get me out of here, I thought. Static crackled in my head like a radio stuck between stations. The halls began to clear and my locker materialized — finally. As I twisted the combination lock, I heard across the way, "So, you just transferred? Where'd you go before here?"

I opened the door and captured Brandi and Cece in my mirror.

Cece said, "Washington Central."

Brandi said, "Oh, yeah? Do you know Joanie? She's one of us. Joanie Fowler."

"Doesn't sound familiar."

"You have to know her."

"I said I don't." The sharpness of Cece's voice made me turn around. Brandi caught my eye and I turned back. In my mirror I watched as Cece shoved a book into her backpack and removed a fleece vest off the hook. She let out a long breath and said, "Sorry," to Brandi. "It's been a rough day."

"I can imagine." Brandi smiled knowingly. I wondered what she knew. Brandi held the backpack while Cece put on her vest. Their conversation muted as a herd of people stampeded past. I caught the tail end of Brandi's ". . . go for a Coke or something?"

"I can't," Cece said. "I have to work." She retrieved the pack from Brandi and slung it over her shoulder. I realized I was eavesdropping shamelessly and squatted to unzip my swimming duffel.

"How come you transferred?" Brandi asked.

"Health reasons." Cece slammed her locker. "My car wouldn't

start this morning and I don't really want to wait here for my brother to pick me up. Do you think you could give me a ride to work?"

"Sure," Brandi chirped. "No problem." They headed out together.

Brandi had said, "One of us." Did that mean she was gay?

Huh. I didn't think we had any gays in our school. Until now.

I loaded up my backpack and grabbed my duffel, thinking, I guess it pays to advertise.

Chapter 2

As I dragged in the back door at home, Mom called, "Holl, is that you? I need you." I dumped my stash on the landing and followed her voice to the living room. "Oh, good," Mom said. "Could you finish feeding Hannah for me? I have *got* to pee."

I relieved her of the baby and the bottle. "Hello, Hannie," I cooed, lifting her in the air so she'd grin dimples at me. So cute. Settling her in the crook of my arm, I inserted the nipple between her gooey lips, then crossed the room to sprawl on the sofa. I propped Hannah against my bent knees. She suckled and flapped her chubby arms, making me laugh. God, she was precious. Sometimes it felt as if she were mine.

Mom padded in, breathing relief and refastening the jaw clip in the back of her hair. Flopping into the armchair, she asked, "How was your day?"

"Good." I let Hannah's tiny fingers curl around my thumb. "How was yours?"

"Exhausting. Did you stop in to see Bonnie Lucas? I asked her to get you a few more catalogs and applications — just in case."

"Oh, damn." My head fell back against the armrest. "Sorry, I forgot." "In case" meant in case Vassar and Brown rejected me like Harvard had. Those colleges were way out of my league, but try to tell my mother that. She forced me to apply for early decision, even though I could've told her what the decision would be. Early or late.

"The deadline for filing applications at most other schools is February first, Holland," she said. "That doesn't give us much time. And you don't want to settle for some in-state school like Metro Urban." She wrinkled her nose.

"I'll go in tomorrow. Would you toss me that towel?" Hannah's drool was stringing to her chest.

Mom got up and handed me the towel off her shoulder. "Faith is coming this weekend."

"Again? We just got rid of her."

"Holland," Mom chided.

"Well, I'm sorry but —" I bit my tongue. She'd heard it all before.

Faith was my wicked stepsister, if I had to claim her as a relative. She was a walking freakshow. Currently, she was into Goth, which was just sick after Columbine. We'd bonded like repelling magnetic poles. Neal, my new stepdad, introduced us only a few weeks before his and Mom's wedding, and I knew instantly we weren't going to be playing one-big-happy. I could tolerate Faith, barely, every other weekend, but after Hannah arrived and Mom converted my bedroom into a nursery, Faith and I had to share bedroom space downstairs. At my murder trial, the jury would find that the defendant had a case for justifiable homicide.

Not a lot of people got under my skin, but Faith did and she knew it. Knew it and used it.

I ran my knuckles across Hannah's silky cheek, wondering if I'd ever had such flawless skin.

Mom perched on the sofa arm, fanning her fingers up through my bangs. "I know how you feel about Faith, but she's young."

"She's fifteen." Under my breath, I added, "Going on six."

Mom sighed. "I appreciate your patience with her."

Like I had any.

"It won't be long now. You'll be leaving soon enough for college. Too soon." Mom tweaked my nose. She reached over to pluck Hannah off my stomach and asked, "Where's Seth going? Has he decided?"

"Stanford, last I heard." It was a subject we avoided like the plague. Seth wanted us to go to the same college, the probability of which was less than zero given the fact he could pick and choose. Seth had goals. He was going to be a microbiologist. By age twenty-five he'd be happily married with two point five kids, a dog, a three-car garage — the whole Big Mac with cheese. He said he couldn't stand the thought of us being separated for four years, that even if we didn't get into the same college we should try to stay close. As in proximity. He'd been pressing me to commit. To something, anything.

I rolled off the sofa and pushed to my feet. Stretched my back and yawned.

Mom said, "Did you get a new work schedule?"

"Not yet. I need to find out about swim team practices. I'll do that tomorrow, too." Trailing Mom and Hannah to the kitchen, I thought out loud, "God, I have a shitload of homework."

Mom twisted and frowned at me.

"Sorry, Hannie." I cupped my hands over her tiny ears. "You didn't hear Sissy's gutter mouth."

Mom evil-eyed me, but couldn't suppress her grin.

"Tell me again why I have to take so much crap this semester?" I lugged my duffel up to one stiff shoulder, my backpack to the other.

"Because you're going to need a scholarship. It isn't fair to expect Neal to pay for your college education, and what I've saved wouldn't cover one semester at Harvard."

Which she didn't have to worry about, since they declined my offer to sweep their hallowed halls for a mere forty grand a year.

"Those classes will look good on your transcript," Mom said. "Show you're serious."

"About majoring in masochism?"

She ignored me. "It'll put you that much further ahead. Oh, and ask Bonnie to loan you that book on private scholarships again, will you? Just in case."

Just in case I'm a universal reject.

"Holland?" Mom called at my back. "I was at the pharmacy picking up my prescription and they gave me yours by mistake."

My face flared.

"It's on your desk. You can pay me back out of your next paycheck."

I mumbled, "Okay, thanks," and sprinted down the stairs. If she had her suspicions about Seth and me before, they were now confirmed. The crypt, otherwise known as my basement bedroom, was dim even with all the lights on. Mom and Neal had tried to transform it into a cozy little cubbyhole, with curtains and bookshelves and partitions between our bedrooms. But it'd always be "the unfinished basement" to me.

It wasn't that I resented giving my old room to Hannah; it was having to share my privacy with the goddess of Goth. "Every *other* weekend," I reminded the holy rafters, drafty though they were. If Faith was going to be hanging around here that often, my friends would get their fill of me.

Sighing, I flung my pack on the bed and started stripping. The white pharmacy bag on the desk begged attention, so I snatched it up and carted it to the bathroom, ripping it open. Wow, I'd even forgotten to stop by after school and pick up my pills. I didn't remember calling in the refill, and my period ended two days ago. I *was* a wastoid.

I popped out Monday and Tuesday. Caught up. Wouldn't Mom have a hemorrhage if I got pregnant in high school, too? She'd kill me. She had plans for Holland Jaeger. And they didn't include what Holland Jaeger wanted. Whatever that was. I threw on my grubby sweats and settled in for the duration.

▼▲▼

The ringing of my cell phone jerked me out of *Beowulf.* I dog-eared the page and riffled through my bag, catching the phone on the fourth ring. "Hello?"

"Babe, you need a study break?" Seth said in his most suggestive voice.

"Yeah, but if we do that, I'll never get back into it."

He chuckled. "Can I come over?"

I checked the time. Twenty to eleven. "For a little while. I haven't even started my calc problems."

"See you in ten," he said and hung up.

I refolded the phone and resumed reading. A few minutes

later, a rap sounded on the basement window. I leapt off the bed and sprinted up the stairs, where Seth's face materialized in the back door window.

He took one step inside and peered into the kitchen. "Is Neal here?" he whispered.

"No, he's in Baltimore on business," I whispered back.

"The dragon lady asleep?"

I nodded.

Seth wiggled his eyebrows.

"I mean it, Seth. Not long, okay?"

He tiptoed down the stairs behind me.

We'd gotten very good at fast and soundless sex. Maybe after a year it was supposed to be that way. Easy. Rehearsed. He took off a little before midnight, leaving me with another two hours of homework. New rule, I decided. Not on a school night. And that included Sunday. Wouldn't my mother be proud?

Chapter 3

Somebody splashed acid in my eyes — at least that's what it felt like. I dug around in my duffel for the case and removed my contacts. Sure, you could swim with contacts in, if you didn't mind going blind. Shit. Now I'd have to wear my glasses all day. I should've searched harder for my goggles this morning.

The locker across from me clanged open and I blinked up to my mirror. There she was, clutching a mega cup of coffee in her left hand, a donut between her teeth. As she reached down for something in her locker, she disappeared from view.

"Ow, ow, shit!"

I whirled. The plastic lid on her cup had fallen off and scalding coffee had poured down her arm. She was hopping around, holding her wrist. I unzipped my duffel and yanked out the first wet thing on top, then charged over and slapped it up against her arm. "Here, use this."

"Owww," she yowled.

I winced, knowing how that hurts. "Let me see. You could have third-degree burns."

She loosened the makeshift bandage and peered at her arm. Good, no blisters. Rash red, though. She smelled spicy, like cinnamon.

I glanced up to see her looking at me, hard. "Do you always carry around a wet swimsuit?" she asked. She indicated her arm, where I'd rewrapped my Speedo.

"You never know when you might need one."

She laughed. Infectious.

"Thanks, Holland." She removed the suit. Tried to. My hands were gripping her arm so hard she had to pry them loose.

"Sorry." I let go fast. Rewind. Replay. She knows my name.

"I can't believe I did that." She rubbed her arm. "How am I going to get through the morning without coffee?" Holding the now empty cup, she retrieved chunks of coffee-soaked donut and dropped the soggy mess into the cup.

"There's a coffee machine in the cafeteria," I told her.

"Yeah?" Her eyes lit up. "Thanks. You're a lifesaver." She plucked my swimsuit off the floor and held it up by the crotch. "Literally."

I snatched it away and she smirked. Returning to my locker, I jammed the suit into the duffel and rezipped it.

"Where do you swim?"

I sprang upright. She'd followed me and was leaning against the locker next to mine.

"In the pool." Well, duh, Holland. Dazzle her with your brilliant repartee. "The school's pool. Downstairs. Open swim begins at six and I can get a few laps in before first hour. *My* morning cup of coffee."

Her eyebrows arched. "You're seriously demented."

My stomach jumped. I wished it'd stop doing that.

"I'm Cece Goddard." She stuck out her hand.

"I know. Holland —"

"Jaeger. I know." We both let out little laughs, nervous like, then shook hands. She said, "You're student body president."

"How did you know that?"

She shrugged. "I asked around."

"Babe, hey." Seth's voice echoed down the hall. I realized I was still holding Cece's hand and dropped it fast. Why? We were just getting acquainted. He sauntered down the hall, a tower of books under his arm. His free hand snaked around my waist and pulled me into him. "Long time no do this." He bent down and kissed me.

Out of the corner of my eye, I saw Cece push off.

Seth finished with me and said, "Come on. I'll walk you to class."

I hauled down my lit and calc books, which Seth took and added to his stack. At the end of the hall, I glanced back over my shoulder to see her headed in the opposite direction.

She'd asked around. Huh. Why would she do that?

▼▲▼

We headed toward the parking lot at lunchtime to rendezvous with everyone else at my Jeep. We'd decided to eat off campus at least a couple of days a week. On the way, I informed Seth of my no-school-night rule. He wasn't pleased. "I'll see what I can do about borrowing the Regal Friday night," he said.

"No, Seth. You know I hate doing it in your dad's car."

"Okay, I'll check to see if the villa's free."

He was mad. Great. "I'm sorry, but it's just gross."

"Then your place."

"Neal's coming back tomorrow," I told him.

Seth sulked all the way to Taco Bell. He didn't mind doing it right under my mother's nose, but horrors my stepfather should catch us. What was that, some kind of guy thing? Granted, Neal was the size of a linebacker, but underneath the blubber, he was a big teddy bear. Seth knew that.

He was still sullen half an hour later when we got back to school. "I hate this," he said, stalling at the door after the others had gone in.

"Yeah, me too."

He lifted my chin with a finger. "Let's just get married."

"Okay. After econ, though, because I have an assignment to turn in. And we're not consummating the union in your dad's Regal."

Seth blinked. "You're assuming we'd make it out of the church."

I kicked him and he wrestled me into his arms.

▼▲▼

I resumed my same seat in art. I always do that, pick a spot the first day and never move. What does that say about me? Boring and predictable. Everyone else had shifted around. Winslow, geek-cum-punk, slid in beside me. "Yo," he said.

"Yo yourself," I said back.

She wasn't in her seat. I scanned the studio and located her a couple of tables over, by the picture window. She was turned away from me, gazing outside.

Look at me, I thought. Look at me, look at me, LOOKATME.

God, Holland. Shut it off. What was *that* about? I concentrated on doodling in my spiral. Concentrated on not looking at her.

Mackel rushed in, balancing a stack of videotapes on a slide carousel. "Sorry I'm late." He dumped the load on his desk. "Roll call. Everyone here? Good." He opened a drawer and pulled out a ream of blank newsprint. "Pass these around," he said, splitting the paper between the front two tables. "My stash of pencils has gone AWOL, so use whatever you've got. Pencil, pen, lipstick."

As Winslow passed me a sheet of paper, I saw Mackel drag a tall stool over to the front and set an apple on the seat. "Draw this," he said, spreading his arms dramatically over the stool.

I panicked. If this is a test, I thought, I'm toast. It took a while to focus my attention on the task at hand, distracted as I was by Brandi passing Cece a pencil and Cece smiling thanks. She had a nice smile. I wondered how her arm was, if I should ask. Ask why she asked around about me. I studied the assignment. Granny Smith apple. Sour. My mouth watered. The best ones for pies, though, Mom always said.

A few minutes into it, my cell rang. "Shit," I hissed under my breath. I must've forgotten to turn it off. Naturally, the phone had fallen to the bottom of my bag, under layers of detritus. It rang and rang. I finally fished it out. "What?"

"Hey, babe."

"Seth, I'm in class," I whispered and ducked my head, as if that was going to make me invisible.

"So am I," he whispered back. "I just wanted to tell you I'm sorry about earlier. About being such a grump."

"It's all right."

"I love you."

"Yeah, me too. Hang up, goon." I folded the phone. "Sorry," I said to Mackel, and all the other people around me who were gawking. Including Cece. I rolled my eyes and she grinned.

It took me a minute to remember the assignment. Get going again. Once I concentrated my energies, time flew. Mackel stood up. "Okay," he said, startling me. "Sign your masterpieces somewhere, front preferably, with your own name preferably, and hand them in. You won't get graded. I just want first crack at the next budding Picasso."

I glanced over my drawing. Not bad. I'd captured the essence of form, anyway. I watched as her essence of form exited the door with Brandi.

▼▲▼

We had a student council meeting after school. I called the meeting to order, then deferred to our new faculty advisor, Mr. Olander. He asked us to introduce ourselves, tell what class we were in, what office we held. Seth he already knew. Probably from bio or something, since Mr. Olander was the new head of the science department.

Seth ended his spiel with, "And I'm Holland's vice," which cracked everyone up. I'm not sure Olander got it. He was going to be as fun as a box of mold.

The council was composed of six class representatives, plus officers. Kirsten was secretary. Olander asked her to please read the minutes of the last meeting we'd held before break. She did, then flipped her steno pad, and added, "Oh, and we voted. It was unanimous. Our new faculty rep would have to strip to his tighty-whiteys and do the chicken dance at an all-school assembly."

We all smothered grins.

Olander's eyes about shattered his spectacles.

Kirsten said to him, "Joke."

"Oh." He chortled. "Ha. Good one."

Oy. I took back the meeting from Clueless Guy. "Community Service Week is coming up in February," I announced. "What do we want to do this year?"

Kirsten piped up, "Condemn the cafeteria? That'd be a service to the community."

Everyone laughed. Kirsten huffed. "Hey, I'm serious."

Right. We brainstormed ideas that were actually doable and settled on a blood drive, a canned-food collection for the homeless shelter, and a read-a-thon for local nursing homes. Same as last year. How boring and predictable is that?

On the way out, Kirsten snagged me and said, "Leah told me to tell you that Mrs. Lucas was still looking for you."

"Damn." I smacked my head. Kirsten added, "If you go to the career center, would you pick me up a catalog for Western State? Thanks." She jogged over to Trevor, who was waiting for her by the office. Trevor. He must've been her third or fourth boyfriend this year. I watched as she practically mauled him against the trophy case. He looked so young. But then he would, considering he was a freshman. I wondered if I should tell her what people were saying. Suggest maybe she cool it in school.

Seth came up behind me and poked me in the ribs. I yelped and slapped him away. "Keep Friday night open," he murmured in my ear. "I have a solution to our problem." He swaggered away toward the chem labs.

I scanned the back of his long, lean frame, letting out an audible sigh. One thing about Seth — he had a solution for everything.

Chapter 4

Snow was beginning to stick to the asphalt in the school parking lot. My Jeep was already filmed over with frozen sleet. Mom said I was nuts to buy such a hunk of junk, and at the moment, shivering under the ripped canvas cover, I had to agree. But it'd been a blast all summer, four-wheeling the ridgeback.

My bones were brittle by the time I swerved into Children's Cottage. "Holland, thank God." Judy Arndt rushed up to meet me at the door. "Could you watch Dinosaur Digs while I run this money to the bank before it closes?"

"Sure."

"You're a saint." She slipped out behind me, skittering down the icy wheelchair ramp.

Unzipping my hooded sweatshirt, I hustled up the hall toward the pre-K room, admiring the miniature marshmallow art on the walls as I went. "Miss Holland! Miss Holland!" a couple of kids shrieked when they saw me at the door.

"Hi, Courtney. Stef." They raced over and flung their arms

around me. "Ooh, Steffi, I love your princess outfit." She beamed and twirled around for me. The other kids were trying on costumes from the make-believe trunk, or building with LEGOs, or bopping out at the karaoke center. There was another aide in the room, Mrs. Ruiz, Courtney's grandma, who volunteered a couple of days a week. We greeted each other with smiles as she divvied up Teddy Grahams for snack time. Courtney and Stef ran back to the mirror.

"Come and play with us, Miss Holland," Kyle hollered across the room. Everyone else looked busy, so I joined him and his brother, Kevin — the twin terrors.

This had to be the best job in the world. Yeah, it was minimum wage, and it was tough to put in even ten hours a week with my schedule, but I'd sacrifice swim team before giving this up. I loved little kids. They were so funny, so real. The way they'd crawl into your lap or hang off your neck. Sometimes they were pretty needy, like they weren't getting much affection at home. That was fine with me. I had plenty of love to spread around.

Courtney snuck up behind me and smashed sticky fingers over my eyes. "Guess who?" she said.

"Barney?"

"No."

"Scooby Doo?"

She giggled. "No."

"The Three Little Pigs?"

"It's me!"

I grabbed her and tickled her in my lap. I wanted a hundred kids, at least.

Mom was hanging up the phone when I blew in the back door a little after six. "That was Bonnie Lucas."

I grimaced. "Mom —"

"No excuses," she said. "Get in there tomorrow. She's gone to a lot of trouble sending away for those catalogs and applications. I went ahead and filled out the financial aid forms you left sitting on your dresser."

"Mother." Involuntarily, my fists clenched. I wish she'd stay out of my room. Better yet, out of my life. I drew a deep, calming breath before kissing Hannah in her baby seat. Mom nudged me away and lifted Hannah up, adding, "You act like you don't even care."

"I care," I said, bristling again. Why didn't *she* go to college if she was so psyched about it?

I yanked open the fridge and snitched a bowl of leftover chicken. Selected a bag of chips off the counter for dessert. Down in the crypt I punched on my CD player and changed into sweats, then dumped books and notebooks out on my bed. This sickening feeling of dread seeped up from my core. It'd been festering for a while now. Why did I have to go to college? I loved school, but mostly for the social life. I couldn't imagine another four years poring over textbooks and writing reports and giving presentations and staging all-nighters.

Shoving the books aside, I rolled over and hugged my pillow. What was wrong with me? Ever since senior year started, I just couldn't get motivated. Couldn't get into it. Time seemed to have sped up and taken off without me. Or stopped altogether. This sense of inertia encased me in amber. Sometimes I'd catch myself looking at my reflection in windows and wonder who I was. Where I was going. Then the image would change and it wouldn't be me, just some nebulous shadow person. An empty, spineless shape-shifter.

Mom's footsteps creaked upstairs in my old bedroom. A pang of guilt stabbed me in the gut. I knew why she was so obsessed with college. She would've gone if she could have, but she'd dropped out of high school when she got pregnant with me. She had to. Her parents kicked her out. She never talked much about those years. We lived in a shelter for a while, I think. Eventually Mom got into a program for unwed mothers and earned her GED. Attended trade school and worked as a paralegal.

I admired her, I really did. She'd been through a lot. She was strong and independent, much more so than me. One time, while she was pregnant with Hannah, I went with her for an ultrasound and I remember sitting in the doctor's office, Mom leafing through a parenting magazine, both of us cooing over the cute baby clothes. She told me she'd regretted having me so young, that she would've been a better parent had she waited and planned. I tried to tell her she was a great mom, but I don't think she heard me. Or believed it. She said if she'd been older, more mature, she might've wanted me more.

I squeezed my eyes shut, banishing the memory, the implication. Hannah was wanted. I wasn't.

I should've been resentful of Hannah, and maybe I was, at first. But Mom shared her with me. It was like we were raising Hannah together. I loved that, the teamwork. And nobody could hold a grudge against a baby, especially a cutie patootie like Hannah.

My cell rang, jolting me back to the present.

"Hi, Holl," Seth said. "You busy?"

"Extremely," I informed him. "Don't even think it. I need my sleep."

"Hmmm. I always sleep better afterwards."

"Yeah, well, you pretty much sleep through it."

"Hey!"

"Kidding," I said.

"Listen, about Friday night. It's off. My brother and his roommates were going up skiing the whole weekend and said we could use the apartment, but now one of them has to work." He sighed heavily. "I'm sorry."

"That's okay." For some reason I felt relieved.

"They rescheduled for the weekend after, so we'll have the place to ourselves then. Meanwhile, I guess it's get down and dirty in dungeonland."

"Neal's home for the rest of the month," I told him. "And Faith's here this weekend."

Seth muttered a curse.

"You're just spoiled because of vacation."

"No shit," he replied. "I think I'm addicted. Addicted to you."

"They have medication for that."

He chuckled. "Hey, Echo Lake's opening Saturday. Want to go skating?"

"Yeah." I perked up. "I'll call Leah and Kirsten. We haven't all gone out since summer."

"Oh, all right," Seth said flatly.

"If you don't want me to —"

"No, it's fine. We just never seem to do anything alone anymore."

That wasn't true. He had me to himself all the time.

He added, "Have you thought anymore about," his voice lowered, "the big C?"

My jaw clenched. "I think I hear my mother nagging."

"Holl —"

"Seth, as soon as I know, you'll know. I promise."

And when will that be? I asked myself. The answer was obvious: As soon as I figured out where my mother's life ended and mine began.

Chapter 5

The contacts had to go. Why I'd wanted them in the first place — oh, yeah. To accentuate my extraordinary beauty. Who was I kidding?

My hair was still damp as I pushed through the door of the girls' locker room. A blast of frigid air met me as Coach Chiang materialized in the doorway from the faculty parking lot. "Holland," he called. "Just the person I wanted to see."

I waited for him to catch up. "Would you swim the two-hundred med relay?" he asked. "Claire broke her arm snowboarding over the weekend, and our first meet's Friday. I'd hate for the team to have to withdraw."

"Ouch." I winced for Claire. Then for me. "Coach, you've seen my 'fly. Are you that desperate?"

"'Fraid so."

I rolled my eyes. "Okay, but only for the glory of Southglenn High."

He punched my arm and disappeared into the boys' locker room. I sprinted up the stairs. She was already at her locker, her mega cup of coffee balanced on a box of donuts by her feet. She had earphones on and as she pulled a book off the shelf, she started rocking out. The way you do when no one's around.

It made me laugh.

Her eyes flew open and she smiled, did a one-eighty.

I mouthed, What are you listening to?, indicating the earphones. I dropped my duffel next to my locker.

Cece boogied across the hall and lifted one ear flap for me to listen. I had to lean in to hear and our faces accidentally touched. We both jerked away, as if we'd been shocked. She yanked off the earphones and clipped them onto my head.

I didn't recognize the song. I pressed my hands over my ears to drown out the white noise, while Cece stood with her CD player, nodding in time with the imagined beat. Great group — girl singers. The rhythm was contagious and made me want to dance. So I did. I spun my combination lock and swung open the door at the same time. When the song ended, I handed the earphones back to Cece. "They're good," I said. "They sound kind of familiar. Who are they?"

"Dixie Chicks. Here, listen to this one." She popped the earphones back on me and slid in another CD with a homemade label. It was a different group, heavy metal. The kind of stuff Seth likes. I must've made a face because Cece started laughing.

I pulled down the earphones. "What?"

"That's my brother's band," she said. "Bad, aren't they?"

"Not that bad."

"Liar."

I handed her back the earphones and she returned to her

locker. She called across the hall, "You want a donut? I've got plenty."

My gaze fell to the box on the floor. "Hot 'N Tott Donuts," it read across the side. "No, thanks." The warning bell rang and I hustled to gather my morning books together. A brief glance in my mirror caught Cece staring at me as she sipped her coffee. My stomach did that thing.

I slammed my locker and spun around, colliding with a mass of bodies. My armload of books went flying. The bodies were all jocks dressed in gym shorts, apparently heading out to the track. A couple of them stopped and apologized, helped retrieve my stuff. Cece, I noticed, just stood there and watched.

Dammit, I thought, this is your fault. Get your butt over here and help.

She must've read my expression because she wandered across and said, "Any of you guys want a donut?"

Like vultures, they shoved the books at me and attacked the donut box. I shot Cece a sneer and she laughed.

▼▲▼

Mackel handed back our drawings. There was a sticky note on mine that said, "See me after class." My pulse quickened. Was he going to make me drop? I should have. He could obviously tell I was just filling the hour.

It wasn't helping my anxiety level to see that Brandi had seated herself next to Cece again. Or had Cece saved the seat? Cece was showing Brandi her drawing and giggling. They both were. So what? Why did that rag me? Winslow was chuckling and showing me his drawing, which looked like a two-year-old's. At the top of Winslow's paper Mackel had written, "Interesting minimalist interpretation." It wasn't like I was jealous or anything. Why would I be? Cece had a right to choose her own friends. I just wished she'd choose me.

Shut up, brain.

Mackel launched into an explanation of all the various uses of pencils and charcoal and markers, then demonstrated the effects you could achieve with each. I tried to take notes, but wasn't exactly sure what to write down. He told us as soon as we bought our supplies to play around with them, get a feel.

I waited for the room to clear before approaching Mackel. He glanced up from his desk, where he was checking off names with abandon on the attendance sheet. He smiled, blankly.

"You wanted to see me?" I showed him my drawing.

"Ah, yes. I almost forgot." He studied my page for a few seconds before looking back at me. Cocking his head.

Oh, God, I thought. Don't get mad. Please don't get mad. I hate it when people get mad at me.

"What are you doing in here?" he asked.

My face fried. "I, uh, just needed one more elective before graduation and —"

"Shouldn't you be in advanced drawing?"

"Huh?"

Springing to his feet — giving me a heart attack — he hefted himself onto the desk and hugged one leg. "Come on," he said. "Who are you kidding?"

I gulped a lemon. "Apparently not you." I added quickly, "I don't know what you mean."

"This apple." He pointed to my drawing.

"Yeah?"

A smile streaked across his face. He jumped down, giving me more heart palpitations, then riffled through a portfolio on his desk, found what he was looking for, and cleared the desk. Next to my drawing, he laid out three or four others. "Notice anything?"

I skimmed the pictures. "Not really."

He frowned a little. "You can't see the difference?"

I could. I mean, mine was . . . comprehensive. Along with everyone else I'd drawn the apple. Then it dawned on me. "Oh, you *only* wanted the apple?"

Mackel threw back his head and laughed.

No fair. "I thought you wanted the stool and the desk and the easel behind it . . ."

Mackel slapped his forehead. "My God, she doesn't even know she's a genius."

My eyes fell. "Get real." Did he mean it? I compared my drawing to the others again. It *was* better. More realistic looking. I'd done some drawing on my own over the years, just fooling around, sketching animals and people. I never thought of myself as an artist.

Mackel glanced at the name on my paper and said, "Holland." He raised his bushy head. "You really should consider transferring to a higher class. Level II or III."

"Do I have to?"

"No, but I don't know how much you're going to get out of Drawing I. Besides the basics."

I thought about it. Not for long. "I'll stay. I need the basics. I'm sure I'll learn something." I reached for my drawing.

He snatched it off the desk. "Please," he said, clutching my paper to his chest. "May I keep this? As the first of your magnificent masterpieces?"

He was so weird. "Hey," I waved him off, "line your birdcage."

He gasped. "I shall treasure this always."

Nutcase, I decided as I scuttled out of there. Totally devoid of frontal matter.

▼▲▼

Mom called me at lunchtime to remind me to stop by the career center. Why didn't she just buy me a beeper, or one of those electronic devices convicts wear on their ankles? She also told me I had an envelope waiting at home. I could tell by her barely concealed excitement that she'd either opened it or knew what it contained. She disconnected before I could ask.

Mrs. Lucas was in a meeting when I arrived at the career center. Her door was ajar, and I heard the principal, Mr. Reynardi, snarl, "That kid's dangerous. I don't want him in this school. If you don't do it, Bonnie, I'm calling the cops." He charged out, almost bulldozing me down. "Excuse me," he mumbled.

I'm glad I wasn't the subject of *that* discussion.

"Holland, there you are." Mrs. Lucas bustled out of her office. She looked frazzled, as usual. "I have a box of goodies for you. Catalogs and applications, financial aid forms and resource books. Did you get your invite?"

"My what?"

She clapped a hand over her mouth. "I didn't say that."

I eyed the box on a folding chair near her door and heaved a sigh. More audible than it was meant to be.

Mrs. Lucas furrowed her brow. "You okay? You look tired." She reached for my cheek.

I backed away and forced a smile. "I'm fine. I'll just take this stuff. Oh, do you have a catalog for Western State?"

"You're not thinking of going there?" She looked aghast.

"It's not for me. It's for Kirsten."

"Oh. Well." She walked past me to the door, where the catalogs for the state schools were stacked along the wall.

Accompanying me down the hall, Mrs. Lucas launched into a lengthy discourse on all the academic scholarships and government grants I could qualify for. How my SATs and ACTs were high enough to get me into most institutions. An institution, I mused, sounded more exciting than college. We reached the main intersection and she added, "On top is the information on schools that offer pre-law programs."

"Pre-law? Who said I wanted to do that?"

"Oh." Mrs. Lucas flinched at the sharpness of my voice. "I thought that was your goal, to attend law school. Your mom said —"

That's all I heard. Muttering a quick thanks I charged off toward my Jeep. To my own space, my own time.

"Holland, wait up," someone called at my back.

I had the exit door scoped out and had to skid to a stop.

"You have a minute?" Cece asked, sidling up beside me.

I glanced at my watch over the two-ton box. Shit, I was already ten minutes late for work. "Sure," I replied, exhaling my frustration.

"You're a terrible liar," she said. "You should work on that."

I sneered at her.

She shouldered her backpack. "What's that stuff?" She indicated the box.

"College crap. You want it?"

"Sure." I wasn't serious, but she relieved me of the box anyway. I might forget she had it. "Where are you going to college?" she asked as we walked together.

"I don't know. I don't know if I even want to go. Where are you going?"

"I'm not sure. Metro Urban, probably. I haven't thought much about it, since I'm only a junior."

"You are?" That surprised me. She seemed so much older. More together.

The second wave of the blizzard that was forecast to sweep in never materialized, but an arctic wind was whipping up eddies of cafeteria debris around the parking lot. Cece, head bent, hurried with me to my Jeep. "Since you're student body president, can you tell me why you don't have a lesbigay club at Southglenn?" She had to raise her voice to be heard over the wind.

"A what?" I yelled.

"Lesbigay," she yelled back.

"A wh —" Oh. It registered. "I guess . . . no one ever applied."

"Well, I want to," she said. "How do I do it?"

We reached the Jeep and Cece balanced the box on the door handle, anchoring her baseball cap on her head with her free hand. "Get in," I said. "We can't talk out here." I unlocked the door and took the box. She climbed in and reached across the seat to unlock my door.

I circled around front and hefted the box into the back, then jumped in and slammed the door. "God, I hate the wind. I don't mind cold, but I hate wind."

"Yeah, me too." Cece scanned the interior, eyes stopping on Seth's camping gear behind my seat. "Is this yours or his?"

"The Jeep? It's mine," I said. "Well, it actually belongs to the bank, but I'm letting them extort money from me for nine or ten more years."

She smiled. "About an LBGT club?" Her eyes rose to meet mine from under the bill of her cap.

"Yeah." I shifted to face her. LBGT. "What's the T stand for?"

"Transgendered," she said. "Should probably add Q for Queer or Questioning. And I for Intersexed."

Intersexed? I'd have to look that one up. "Okay, well, you have to submit an application if you want to form an official school club, which I'm assuming is what you're asking. You'll need to have a mission statement . . ." Why was my heart beating a drum solo? Cold. That was it. I turned on the ignition and revved up the heat. "And you'll need a faculty advisor."

"Like who?"

"Anyone. Anyone who'll agree."

"Why wouldn't they?" she snapped.

"I didn't say they wouldn't," I snapped back. I didn't mean to, it was reflex. "I'm just telling you how to go about it, okay?"

She nodded once, then turned to gaze out the window. "Do you think it'll get approved?" she asked.

"I don't know why not."

She burst into laughter.

"What?"

She twisted back to me and shook her head. "Where do I get an app?"

"I'll get you one. Why do you think it wouldn't get approved?"

Her head tilted to one side. "Oh, I don't know. ESP?"

She was being sarcastic. Why? I mean, we'd never gotten a request for a gay club. Probably because there weren't all that many gays at our school. Two now, counting her. "I'll pick up the form for you tomorrow."

One side of her lip cricked. "Cool."

"Can I take you somewhere?" I checked my watch. Going on twenty minutes late. I hated for Judy to think me irresponsible.

"That's okay," Cece said. "I have my car."

"Which one is it? I'll drive you there."

Cece reached for the door handle. "It's the blue Neon. Parked right here next to you." She shot me a grin and leapt out. I idled in place until she'd gunned her motor and zipped out of the slot. Her rear bumper was crammed with stickers: HATE IS NOT A FAMILY VALUE, GRRLZ KICK AZZ. The frame on her license plate read: 2QT2BSTR8. I had the strongest urge to follow her. More than an urge. A need.

"A need?" I questioned my brain out loud. "Grrl, the only thing you need is to get your azz to work."

Chapter 6

The letter that had come in the mail was an invitation to attend a dinner at the governor's mansion. Apparently I'd been selected to the Governor's Gold Circle, which honored the top high school scholars in the state.

"Wow," Neal exclaimed at dinner, passing the invitation back to Mom. "How'd you rate that?"

"My question exactly."

"Neal," Mom scolded him. "In case you hadn't noticed, my daughter is brilliant."

"Get real, Mom. I don't even have a four-oh."

"It's not all based on GPA," she said. "You have to demonstrate community service and leadership skills. Your participation in sports was a bonus. Not to mention that Bonnie was on the nominating committee."

"Mom! God. Did you put Mrs. Lucas up to this?"

"Of course not." Mom looked offended. "It was her idea."

I bet, I thought, gritting my teeth.

Mom inserted the invitation back into its crisp envelope,

running her index finger across the raised governor's seal. "You'll need something new to wear," she said. "A dress. Not pants." Mom handed me the letter.

I snatched it from her and tossed it onto the credenza behind me. "I haven't decided if I'm going. Anyway, it's not until March."

"Of course you're going."

Hannah fussed and Mom spooned another glop of liquified turkey into her mouth.

"I have a better idea." I scraped back my chair and stood. "You go. The governor'll like you better, I'm sure."

"Holland —" The hurt in Mom's voice stopped me. Without turning around, I said, "Mom, just let me make my own decisions, okay? I think I'm old enough now." I twisted to meet her eyes. "Don't you?"

Deadpan, she said, "You make me sound like some kind of horrible, meddling mother."

Neal snorted. I appealed to him, but he threw up his hands and said, "Hey, I'm out of this one."

Mom urged another spoonful of turkey into Hannah's mouth. "I trust you to make your own decisions, honey. You'll do the right thing. You always make me proud."

Tears filled my eyes. Charging down the stairs, I screamed inside, When? When, Mom? When have I ever made you proud? Never. If I work my butt off to get straight A's, I'm not taking hard enough classes. If I swim a personal best, I should've chosen a sport where my best would be good enough to win. I should get a better job, a better car, a better grip on my reality.

Mom had looked shocked when I told her I got elected student council president, like I couldn't possibly have achieved anything so impressive on my own. The one choice I'd made in my life that she approved of was Seth. She was gaga over Seth.

Shit. I'd go to the stupid dinner. But hell would have to freeze over before I ever wore a dress.

▼▲▼

I stalled around at my locker waiting for Cece, watching the time. I'd cut my laps short so I could run to the office and pick up a club application for her. It was getting late. I didn't dare linger past the warning bell for fear of Arbuthnot. The bloody wrath of Arbuthnot. Earlier this week she'd verbally bludgeoned a girl to tears for being two minutes late. She'd ranted on and on about being responsible, showing respect for her, for our peers, for all of us who made the effort to be here on time. Needless to say, the girl dropped the class. A lot of people had dropped. I would've too, if I didn't need another lit credit to graduate.

The bell rang. No Cece.

After lunch I sprinted up the stairs to art. She was sitting at the table nearest the window, talking to Brandi. Some compulsion drove me to interrupt their little tête-à-tête. "Cece?"

She blinked up at me. "Yeah?"

"I have this application for you." I searched my stack of spirals to find it. Ignoring me, Brandi continued, "So, anyway, if you want to come over tonight I could pick you up after work."

"Here." I shoved the app at Cece.

"Okay, thanks." She smiled and laid it on top of her books. To Brandi she said, "I'll call you."

Mackel flew in the door. "Heads up," he chirruped. "Everybody got their supplies now?"

I stumbled to my table. Winslow was already there, doodling on a tablet. "Yo," he said.

"Yo back." I took a deep breath and tried to clear my head. What was wrong with me? A simmering sort of anger had been festering all morning, even before school started. It began with Mom cornering me in the kitchen to remind me that Faith was staying over this weekend and would I mind not making myself so scarce? Yes, I'd mind. That was the master plan. At the end of class this morning Arbuthnot added *Grendel* to our list of required readings, like I had all this idle time. I couldn't fathom in calculus why we even *had* to learn about rectilinear motion, and if Mackel gave us homework I'd torch his hair.

He must've felt my fire. "We'll do an in-class exercise today," he said. "You should be able to finish it. I want you to create a completely different object out of a familiar one. Alter your mindsets. Expand your vision."

I had no idea what he was talking about. Familiar. I surveyed the room. Everything in here was strange, unsettling. Her, whispering with Brandi. Stop looking at her.

I forced my eyes to the table, to my tablet. My left hand was spread across the paper. Okay. Familiar. I traced around my fingers. Studied the outline.

Turkey. That's all I saw. Winslow reached over and drew the gullet under my thumb. We both cracked up. Had to bury our heads on the table to smother the laughter.

Winslow actually handed in the turkey. I did a pencil scraping over my Jeep key and labeled it, "Not a key. Expand your vision."

On the way to my locker after school my cell rang. It was Seth reminding me about ice skating tomorrow, like I'd spaced it.

Which I had. He said he'd pick me up at ten, then added, "Good luck at your meet. I wish you'd let me come cheer you on."

"Not now. Not ever." We'd been through this. He knew how much I hated people in the audience, how freaked I got knowing someone was out there watching me, expecting me to perform. Swimming wasn't about the competition. It was about . . . I don't know. The team. Me. The girls.

As I slipped my key into the Jeep door, I noticed something stuck under the wiper blade. It was solid and square and wrapped in red foil. Throwing my junk in the back, I clambered onto the seat and shut the door. Running a fingernail under the Scotch tape, I folded back the wrapper and removed the object.

It was a CD. Dixie Chicks. A current of warmth surged up from my core.

▼▲▼

The smell hit me before I got to the basement. "Faith, didn't I ask you not to burn incense down here?" A stick was smoldering on her dresser. Her shrine, I should say. It was littered with all these ghoulish winged creatures, weird religious symbols, and cruci-fixes. The stench of incense permeated everything.

Faith dunked the incense into a glass of water, scowling at me through the mirror. She'd taken extra care to cake on the white makeup. Oh, that didn't bother me as much as the hands she al-ways had in her mouth. She chewed her fingernails until they bled. Apparently Goth advocated self-mutilation.

"Where are you going?" She spit out a cuticle and followed me to the end of the partition separating our spaces.

"Swim meet," I mumbled.

"Can I come?"

Unzipping my duffel, I answered, "You wouldn't want to." I replaced my damp Speedo with a dry one and checked to make sure I had my contact case and goggles. "Ever wonder why we're called the Southglenn Starfish? Because Starfish don't swim." I crossed my eyes at Faith.

She didn't smile. She never smiled. She droned, "It'd be better than staying here with June and Ward Cleaver."

I laughed. Oh, my God. Did Faith have a sense of humor? "I thought you were into torture and sacrifice."

She pivoted and left. Oops. Not funny, the truth. I peered around the partition to tell her it was a joke, but she'd already stuck on her earphones and started fiddling with her CD player. The crap she listened to: Flesh Eaters. Tapping the Vein.

I dug around under my bed for my portable CD player. I hadn't used it in a while. It was dusty. I checked the batteries. At the bottom of the stairs, I heard the strike of a match. Damn her.

▼▲▼

My best event was the fifty freestyle and I still came in dead last. Oh, well. It wasn't like I was bringing down the team — we were all lousy. Our goal, according to Coach Chiang, was to finish out of the toilet, just once.

It was a pipe dream.

Unfortunately, the med relay was scheduled right after my sprint events, and I was so exhausted I barely got off the block before the race was over. As I hauled my dead carcass out of the water, gasping for air and feeling lightheaded, my eyes deglazed on the audience.

Cece was there, standing to the side of the bleachers with a group of girls. No one I recognized. She had on these khaki flight pants and a T-shirt with a check mark. The shirt said, JUST DO IT, and underneath in parentheses, WITH GIRLS. She saw me and hitched her chin up a little in acknowledgment.

If my facial muscles were functional, I might've smiled. What is she doing here? I wondered. Well, duh. She came to see someone swim. Who? Brandi wasn't on the team. Another girl?

I tore off my swim cap and shook out my hair. Soggy and self-conscious, that's how I felt. Coach handed me a towel. "Nice job," he lied.

"They didn't record my time, did they?"

He smiled sheepishly. "'Fraid so. Thanks for filling in, Holland. It's nice to have someone I can count on."

"To swim their personal worst," I muttered, draping the towel over my head. His sneakers squished on the tile as he headed off to BS with the other coach.

"I was getting ready to call out the Coast Guard."

I yanked the towel off my face.

Cece grinned.

"Shut up," I said, and snapped her with the towel.

She caught the end and held it. "We're going to a dance at Rainbow Alley, if you want to come."

"What's Rainbow Alley?" I peered over her shoulder at the girls.

"It's a gay teen center," she said.

A spike of fear lodged in my spine. Why? I wanted to spend time with her, get to know her. But at a gay teen center? What if she thought . . . ? What if it meant . . . ? The static in my head

45

crackled. "Um, thanks, I can't. I have to ride back on the bus with the team." My eyes were drawn to the wet tile under Cece's feet. Unlaced high-tops. How cool.

"I could follow the bus and take you from school," she said.

"I have to get home."

She looked at me. Saw through me. She knew I was lying and wheeled around.

"Cece." I caught her arm. Then dropped it when my hand caught fire. "Thanks for the CD. I played it all the way here. It's awesome."

She smiled again, a slow, suggestive smile. Then she winked and jogged to catch up with her friends.

She was such a flirt. It always made me hurl when girls acted that way. Kirsten, for example. The way she came onto guys. So obvious. With Cece, though, it was different. With her, it was . . . sexy.

Chapter 7

Echo Lake was crowded by the time Seth and I got there. Thank God Faith didn't come. She said she had plans; I imagine they included burning me in effigy. She'd walked in on the rather heated exchange Mom and I were having about me inviting Faith. Sorry, I just couldn't picture Goth on skates. I spotted Leah and Kirsten circling the perimeter of the lake, their heads together, talking. Seth said, "I'm going to go check out the hockey game, see if we can get in." He sprinted for the south shore where an open match was in progress.

I cut across the lake and drew up beside Leah. "Hi, Holl," she greeted me. "How was your meet?"

"Nobody drowned," I said.

"How could you tell if they did?" Kirsten quipped.

Leah whapped her.

"I shouldn't talk." Kirsten refastened the Velcro on her ski mittens. "You couldn't pay me enough to wear a swimsuit in public." Her face suddenly lit up. "There he is. See you guys later." She skated off.

Leah and I watched her speed toward the shore, where Trevor had emerged from the men's room. Wearing hiking boots, I noticed. I arched eyebrows at Leah.

"He doesn't skate," she explained.

"Thank God he's potty-trained."

She smacked me. Kirsten scraped to a stop near the path, spraying Trevor with ice crystals. She threw herself at him, engaging him in a lethal liplock.

"Where did she find this kid?" I asked Leah. "At Toys R Us?"

"Holland, that's mean."

I blanched. "I'm sorry. It's just —" None of my business, that's what it was. So what if Kirsten had worked her way through the seniors and juniors and was starting in on the babies? It was no fuzz off my muff.

"She really loves him," Leah said. "She thinks she's finally found her perfect match."

"Law of averages," I said, "when you strike out that many times."

"Holland." Leah looked shocked.

I winced. "I'm sorry. I'm just being catty. I hope he is the one." We should all find the man of our dreams, I thought.

We glided by the hockey game and Seth called, "Holland. Leah. They're going to need relievers in a couple of minutes. Tell Kirsten to come, too. It's co-ed."

I pulled up at the gate. Leah said, "I'll go tell Kirs. I don't really want to play today."

"You're kidding." I frowned at her.

She took off. Weird. Leah had been dying for the lake to open so we could get up a hockey game every weekend, the way we used to. Was she mad at me now for dissing Kirsten's boyfriend? I was just kidding around, sort of. Geesh.

I tightened my laces and did a couple of knee bends to limber up. As I was slipping my mittens back on, Kirsten sprinted through the gate and scraped up beside me. "Something wrong with Leah?" she asked. "She seems kind of distant lately. Ever since Christmas, really. Have you noticed?"

"Um, yeah." I hadn't, actually. Had I been that self-absorbed? That out of it? Leah was my best friend. I should've noticed.

Kirsten added, "I'm worried about her. She's hardly said three words to me all week." We peered across the lake, where Leah was off by herself skating figures. "Has she talked to you?"

"No," I admitted.

"If she tells you what's wrong, you'll tell me, right?"

"Yeah, of course." Wow. Leah really didn't seem her usual cheery self. "I hope it isn't Conner," I thought aloud.

Kirsten's eyes widened. "No way. They're rock solid."

Conner was Leah's boyfriend. More like fiancé. They weren't officially engaged, but only because they'd decided to wait. Conner was a year older than Leah. After graduation last year he'd joined Americorps and moved to Atlanta. The plan was for Leah to follow in the spring.

I liked Conner, snob that he was. Oh, I just had Beemer envy. The guy was loaded. He'd take Leah out to these romantic restaurants on the weekends when he was in town and drop a hundred bucks on her. A big night out with Seth meant a booth at Wendy's instead of the drive-through.

I hadn't talked to Leah at all beyond our daily lunchtime chatter. Inexcusable. I vowed to catch up soon.

The lodge at Echo Lake provided hockey sticks and helmets, if you didn't bring your own. The blue helmeted goalie raised his hand and called, "Relievers." Three or four players skated to the bench to take a breather.

Helmets were removed and handed around. Kirsten asked, "What color are you, Seth?"

"Blue," he answered. "I'll be goalie, unless you want to."

He was addressing me, but Kirsten piped up, "You go ahead." She snatched the last blue helmet out of my hand. "I'll be your guard, Seth." She winked at him and tossed me her red helmet.

Did she do that on purpose to irk me? Sometimes . . .

Seth crooked a finger my way.

"What?" I selected a hockey stick from the rental rack.

"Come here."

I obeyed. He smooshed my face between his ski gloves. "Good luck," he said. "You're going to need it."

I kissed him, then dug a skate blade into his boot.

The face-off was won by the red team and we jockeyed the puck up ice. The other five players on my team were decent skaters; I'd seen most of them around or played with them before. Coop, one of Seth's friends, was a wing on my team. He acknowledged me with a grunt. The only other girl with a red helmet pulled up beside me, pivoted to skate backward, and said, "Hi. I'm Dayna."

"Holland." We touched gloves.

She reversed direction and charged off toward the net. Wow. With those thighs, she had to be a speed skater.

We blew a scoring opp, but only because Coop and this other

guy on our team hogged the puck. "Over here," I heard Dayna yell more than once, but they wouldn't relinquish control.

Kirsten intercepted a drop pass between Coop and his buddy and sped off toward our goal. Crap.

I caught up with her in the zone and stole the puck back. Took a wide arc and stick-handled the puck down the side, then saw Dayna hailing me and flip-passed the puck over. Coop caught it in the air and hand-passed it to his buddy.

"Dammit," Dayna snarled under her breath as she scraped up beside me. "I had a clear shot."

"I know." We rolled our eyes.

The game went back and forth for the next twenty minutes or so until everyone was pretty wiped. The score was five to four, in favor of the blue team. "Time out," Seth called. The lodge had sent over a vat of hot apple cider and the players swarmed it. I needed to adjust my sock where it was bunching up at the heel. Dayna plopped down next to me on the bench.

"We're taking out Beavis and Butthead," she said. "We'd be up by at least three goals if it wasn't for those jockey jerks."

"No shit," I said. They were totally dominating play.

"If I can ever get the puck, I'm pretty sure I can smoke the red-head."

That was Kirsten. "Okay. I'll do what I can to draw her off. She's got a bad left knee," I told Dayna. "If you can catch her coming around on that side, she doesn't have a quick recovery."

"Yeah?" Dayna's eyes gleamed. "Cool." She crossed one ankle over a knee and cleaned her skate blade. "You're a good player," she said. "You on a team?"

"No. I've been playing in rec league since I was like six. You're a *great* player. Where do you skate?"

"Andersen Rink, at 104th and Sheridan?"

I knew it. Nodded.

"You come here a lot?" Dayna eyed me over her stick.

Before I could answer, Seth skated up with two styrofoam cups of hot cider. "Here, babe." He handed one to me. Noticing Dayna, he offered her the other. What a guy.

"No, thanks," she said, smiling. "You go ahead."

The cider was steaming and spicy and I held it to my face to warm and drift up my nose. Dayna stood, stamped her skates on the ice, and sped off.

I wondered about her. No, I didn't. I knew.

In the second half Dayna bided her time. The hockey jocks not only wouldn't pass, they were hooking and stick checking all over the place. There's no checking in open hockey. Everyone knows that.

A crowd was gathering at the edge and someone called, "You guys about done? We wanna play."

Coop shouted, "One more minute!" He whizzed past me. We were still down a goal. In a blur Dayna bulleted out from behind a blue player and split a seam up the middle. She drove toward Coop's back and body-checked him so hard he went flying. Dayna stole the puck from him and sprinted up the side.

I zipped in behind her. Kirsten passed me by, heading for Dayna, but Dayna crisscrossed in front, almost tripping Kirsten. Dayna took the puck behind the net, going deep. Her eyes darted around until they found me.

I dropped into the slot in front of Seth. He was wary. Seth had great instincts and he knew my best moves. As Dayna drove to the neutral zone, she pivoted and passed to me.

Seth crouched. I deked him and fired in a backhand. Seth dove for it, face first, but the puck slid under him and into the net.

Red team cheered like we'd won the Stanley Cup.

Dayna skated up to me for a high five. As I glided past Seth, still splayed on the ice, I heard him mutter, "Fuck." I bent, picked up the puck, and dropped it on his back. "I think you mean 'puck.'"

He grabbed my ankle and tried to pull me down, but I escaped. He scrabbled to his feet and chased me around the ice, pushing me into a snow bank at the opposite end. We rubbed snow into each other's faces, laughing and wrestling around. Seth pinned my arms and rolled over on top of me. Kissed me. Kept up the pressure until I was struggling to breathe. "Get off," I ordered.

"What?" he said, looking bewildered. He pushed to his knees. "Did I hurt you?"

"No." Yes. I scrambled to my feet. He always has to ruin it, I thought. We could never just have fun.

Coop skated up to us and said to Seth, "We're starting another game. Red team's one short. You or Holland in?"

Seth queried me. "Holl?"

"I'm done," I said, digging snow out of the collar of my parka. "You go on. I need to spend some time with Leah."

He brushed powder off the back of my head, then left.

I found Leah at the outdoor fireplace where she and Kirsten were warming their hands. Leah said, "Good game. I just saw the end where you scored."

Kirsten murmured, "We'd have won if it wasn't for that dyke."

I slowly turned to face Kirsten. "Excuse me?"

She met my eyes and curled a lip.

"If you mean Dayna, she's one hell of an athlete."

Kirsten snorted. "Yeah, they all are."

"What is *that* supposed to mean?"

"Hey." Leah put a hand on my arm. "It's getting cold. Let's go in. Trevor said he'd save us a table in the snack bar."

"Speaking of Trevor," I said, removing my stiff mittens. "People are starting to talk."

Kirsten's head shot up. "About what?"

"Guess."

Her eyes slit. She leaned her face into mine and said, "Why don't you tell me?"

Shit. I shouldn't have started this. She might as well know the truth, though. "They're saying you're a player."

Kirsten expelled a short breath. "Really." Her jaw clenched. "Well, whoever *they* are, they can go fuck themselves." She skated off toward the entrance.

Leah sighed. "Holland —"

"I know." My head lolled back. "Open oven, insert head."

Leah ran her skate blade back and forth along the ice. "She thinks you judge her."

"I don't." Blood rushed to my face. Do I? Maybe I do. "I'm her friend, Leah. I thought she should know. I'm only trying to protect her." Right, Holland. You're so noble. You should alienate your friends with the truth more often. I let out a long, visible breath. "I'll call her tonight and apologize."

"Thank you," Leah said. She hated when brush fires flared between Kirsten and me. Thank God she was always there to douse the flames. It made me wonder how Kirsten and I had stayed friends for so long. We'd known each other since eighth grade, when she and her mom moved here from Texas after her parents first split. Kirs was pretty messed up then. She really wanted to live with her dad, but he'd moved in with his girlfriend and having a kid around would put too much of a crimp in his style. He never called her; not even on her birthday. We got to talking and discovered we had the "fatherless" thing in common.

Kirsten was fun to be around. Wild and crazy, sort of reckless. Unlike me, Ms. Boring and Predictable.

Leah started for the entrance and I caught up. "Are you all right?" I nudged her shoulder with mine. "You seem a little distant, to quote Kirs."

Leah smiled. "I'm fine."

"Sure?"

She opened her mouth, then shut it. Gazing wistfully across the ice, she said, "I miss the old days."

I frowned. "What old days?"

She looked at me. "When we were kids. Coming here. Skating for hours. Playing tag and keep-away. I'm going to miss all this." Her arm extended to include more than the lake.

We dodged a bunch of rowdy boys who were dogging these girls ahead of us. Making them giggle and scream. I guess I knew what Leah meant. Life was easier when we were kids. It wasn't so much about change and choice and moving on. We lived for the moment. Time was eternal.

I linked my arm with Leah's. "Tell you what. I'll buy us a banana split with extra whipped cream and two cherries on top. For old times' sake."

"In your dreams," she said. "I'd have to diet for a week."

▼▲▼

I was just drifting off to sleep Sunday night when Seth called. My eyelids were lead weights after poring over the same page in *Beowulf* six hundred times. Not one word had registered. "Is Faith gone?" he asked.

"Yes." I yawned. "But Neal's here."

"I don't care," Seth said. "I'm coming over."

He hung up before I could protest. Not that I didn't want to see him; but it was Sunday. A school night.

First thing he did after I trailed him downstairs to my room was unzip his jeans. "Jesus, Seth. You didn't even ask."

He paused with his jeans around his hips. "Don't you want to?" he said.

I sighed and plopped on the bed. Scootching up against the headboard, I hugged my knees and answered, "It's not that. I just . . ." I stalled.

"What?" Seth searched my face. "What, Holl?"

"Whenever we're alone, this is all we do."

He rezipped his jeans. Perching on the mattress beside me, he said, "We don't get that much time alone, babe. Since you won't do it in the car and we can't be together when Faith's here. Now school nights are out."

I got the message. "Remember how we used to talk? For like hours and hours, we'd just talk. We never talk anymore."

"We talk every day," he said. "I see you at lunch, and I call you almost every night. We're together on the weekends as much as possible."

I squeezed my eyes shut and dropped my head to my knees. Seth stretched out beside me, snaking an arm around my waist and drawing me close. "We can talk," he said. "What do you want to talk about?"

"I don't know," I murmured.

"I love you," he whispered in my ear. "I know I don't say it enough. I love you, I love you, I love you. Is that what you want to hear?"

It wasn't. I already knew that. "When did we stop being friends?" I raised my head.

He pulled back a little. "We're still friends. You're the best friend I've ever had." He studied me. "It's different with girls, I know. But don't you think of me as your friend?"

"Yeah, I do. Of course I do. It's just . . ." Just what, Holland? Tell him.

Tell him how you want to go back to the way it used to be. Before the sex, the commitment. Oh, yeah. He'd be stoked about that.

Seth kissed my ear, then my neck, my lower neck. Hard as I tried, I couldn't respond to him. What was wrong with me? He was great, wonderful, perfect. He was everything a girl could ever want.

Then why, long after he was gone, did I lie awake and ache inside for something more?

Chapter 8

The cold at first. The swelling of lungs. Then the force. Fighting it, straining against it. Harder, stronger. Glide. Kick. Breathe.

Faster and faster. Moving, moving. Away from it. Toward it. Get there.

My inner voice chanted, "Get there, get there, get there."

Get *where?* I asked.

No answer came.

Concrete grazed my fingertips at the same time my head burst through the surface of the pool. My chest hurt. Every muscle in my body burned. How long had I been swimming? Too long at speed. My eyes stung. I closed them, hung over the edge until the dizziness evaporated. Then I hauled myself out of the pool and padded to the locker room for a hot shower.

"Holland, hi."

I jumped. Usually I was alone at this time of day.

"If I had your self-discipline, I could look like your mother. But alas, my fat cells rebel against shrinkage."

I smiled at Mrs. Lucas. "What are you doing here?" My voice sounded harsh, accusatory. The way I felt — intruded upon.

She didn't notice, unfortunately. Slipping a sweatband over her head, she answered, "We started an early morning faculty shape-up program. Work those biceps." She hefted imaginary weights.

I cursed her silently. My only private time. I really needed to be alone right now. To think. To not think. I grabbed a couple of towels from the laundry cart by the door and headed for the showers. Mrs. Lucas followed. "Did you get through all those catalogs? Have you decided where to apply?"

"Not yet," I told her, screeching on the hot water faucet. "I was swamped with homework all weekend." Which was true. We were only into week two of the term and I was already struggling to keep up. Zero motivation didn't help.

"Well, don't wait too long. Most of those applications have to be postmarked by February first."

"I know," I sniped. Calm yourself, Holland. God. "I'll do it tonight." I twisted my head and smiled at her. Wished her gone.

"Did you get your invitation?"

I didn't answer; just plunged into the shower and zoned.

▼▲▼

Cece was sitting on the floor in front of her locker, poring over an *X-Men* comic book. Her coffee cup was on the carpet next to her, the box of donuts opened to the world. "You're going to get fat," I said before spinning my combination lock out of control. Could I be more surly? I turned to apologize.

Cece hadn't heard, or was ignoring me. I opened my locker

and looked in the mirror. I had to stand on tiptoes to see her. She'd taken a bite of a chocolate donut and was waving it in the air, baiting me.

I smiled to myself. Not to myself. Leaving my locker wide open, I sauntered across the hall and examined the contents of the box. Most of the donuts were broken pieces or misshapen rejects. "These are the poorest excuse for donuts I've ever seen." I squatted and selected a chunk — coconut frosted. "Whatever you paid, you got ripped off."

She closed the comic book. "Since I didn't pay anything, I'd say I got a deal."

"Free donuts?" My eyebrows shot up. "Where?"

"Hott 'N Tott," she said. "My uncle's shop. Or as we fondly refer to it — and to him — Hot to Trot."

I laughed.

She smiled. "I only get them for free because I work there."

My thigh muscles were seizing up, straining on my haunches like this. Up or down? My knees decided. Curling cross-legged on the other side of the donut box, I asked, "Where is this place? Hot to Trot Donuts?"

She cricked a lip. "Over on Speer and Colfax. By Wash Central."

I nodded. Still didn't know where it was. Washington Central was like the netherworld, the other side of the city. The warning bell clanged overhead and I crammed the donut into my mouth. Scrambling to my feet, I darted across the hall.

"Here's the app," she said, suddenly at my side.

"The what? Oh." The "Lesbian Bisexual Gay" title jumped off

60

the top line. I took the club application from her and skimmed over it as I slammed my locker.

"When's your next meeting?" she asked.

"Today, actually." I slid the app into a spiral. "During lunch."

"Okay." We stood there for a moment, sort of awkwardly. My heart was racing. I don't know who moved first, but we began walking down the hall together. Close together. She stopped at the intersection. Or I did. "Let me know what they say," Cece said. "I'll see you in art." She gazed into my eyes, holding me in a trance. When I regained consciousness, she'd retreated. Disappeared into the mist. I drew a deep breath and let it out slowly. Why did she make me feel as if I was teetering on the brink of a precipice? One false step and I'd plunge into the abyss.

▼▲▼

To be different, I decided to hold the student council meeting during lunch at the Pizza Hut across the street. Mr. Olander kicked off the meeting by informing us he'd gotten a request from Admin to help organize a leadership conference at Southglenn in May. We discussed how many rooms to reserve and what topics would be of interest. The details multiplied exponentially as we talked, so I suggested we form a subcommittee. Seth volunteered himself and me to serve on it.

That earned him my most threatening I-wish-you-hadn't-done-that glare. He knew my schedule was already on overkill.

We divvied up duties for the community service projects, too, before Olander said, "Okay, if there's nothing else, motion to adjourn —"

"Wait," I cut in. "There is something." I dug in my backpack for the application. "I got a new club request." I'd shoved it inside my Brit Lit spiral, which lay at the bottom of the stack. "Let me find it."

"What is it this time?" Seth spoke up. "Death Eaters Anonymous?"

A few people laughed. The Goths were the last group to apply for — and be denied — club status, since they couldn't find an advisor. "It's a lesbigay group," I said.

All the air in the room was sucked up.

"The queers want a club? Forget it."

Who said that? My head whipped around. Kirsten?

"Let me see." She snatched the app out of my hand. "Ms. Markenko agreed to be their faculty rep?" She clucked her tongue. "I always figured her for a big dyke."

"Kirsten! God." I yanked the form back.

"Sorry," she said, not sounding it.

"We had this kind of request over at Mitchell, my last school," Olander said.

"What happened?" I asked him.

"Nothing. Too controversial."

My blood boiled. "So we turn clubs down because they're too controversial?"

He looked a little squeamish. "Well . . ."

"Isn't that unconstitutional?" I said. "What about the First Amendment? What about freedom of speech, freedom of association?"

Kirsten replied, "The First Amendment doesn't apply to public school settings, right?" She queried Olander, who looked like he'd rather be pithing a frog than dealing with this.

"Wait a minute —" my voice rose.

Seth reached across the table and squeezed my wrist. "Don't we come off looking like a bunch of intolerant bigots if we turn them down?"

"Thank you," I said to him.

Kirsten quipped, "What do you think Zero Tolerance Policy means?"

A few people sniggered.

I riddled Kirsten with eye bullets. "Very funny."

"Cece Goddard." Kirsten flattened the app on the table to read it upside down. "Who's she?"

"She's new," I said. "She just transferred from Washington Central." To the group, I added, "Obviously they're more progressive there than we are here."

Everyone lowered their eyes, looking embarrassed. They should be. We should be. My eyes focused on Cece's name, then below it to the question: Estimated number of members. Fifteen, she'd written. Fifteen? Did we have that many gays at our school?

Kirsten said, "We're not behind the times, and I don't think we need a gay club at Southglenn. Just because some radical lesbian wants to promote her own agenda, I don't see why we have to comply."

I clucked my tongue. "It's not like that. She doesn't have an agenda. She isn't some kind of militant feminist, or whatever you think. She's cool. She's great." Better shut up, I thought, feeling the heat rising to my face.

Kirsten curled a lip.

"What?" I met her eyes. We had a brief stare-down before Kirsten shook her head and looked away.

Mr. Olander sighed and glanced at his watch. "We have a few minutes. Read the application, Holland."

I read aloud, "Their goal is 'to meet and discuss problems and issues common to the gay community. To socialize. To hold fund-raising events for AIDS and other —'"

Someone murmured, "Next thing you know, they'll want free condoms in the restrooms."

Kirsten's hand shot up. "I'd vote for that."

Everyone howled. Olander said, "I'll check into school policy, but if it's anything like Mitchell, we'll have to deny the request."

"Why?" I screeched. A little too loud, even for my ears.

He replied, "It's too exclusive. If they want a school-sanctioned club, they'll have to open their membership to anyone who wants to join. Not just a select group, like the one they've described. Plus, if they're not sanctioned, they can't do any fundraising on the premises."

Shit. I jammed the app back in my notebook. As we stood to leave, Kirsten asked, "Could we still get the free condoms?"

At the curb, waiting for the crosswalk signal, I cornered her. "Why are you so against this club?"

Kirsten shrugged. "Why are you so for it?"

The light changed and Kirsten took off, not waiting for my answer. Good thing, because I didn't really have one.

▼▲▼

"You'll be keeping a sketchbook to record your daily observations," Mackel told us, slinging a leg over the stool up front. "Don't worry about accuracy or realism. I just want you to focus on everyday things, to see them in a new way. I want you to develop your own approach to art as personal expression."

Personal how? How personal?

My eyes cut to Cece, who was reading her comic book in her lap. How was I going to tell her about the club? Maybe she'd forget to ask. Maybe Harvard would let me in on looks.

Mackel continued, "We're going to do an exercise today in seeing details the way an artist might." He directed someone in the front row to flick off the overhead lights and lower the white screen. Mackel retrieved a remote control for the slide projector, pressed a button, and illuminated the first slide. "What do you see?" he asked.

Someone called out, "A fence."

"Duh," Winslow quipped beside me.

Mackel asked, "What else?"

"Snow."

"And?"

"The void, utter wastelands of our minds," Winslow piped up.

Mackel chuckled. "Better. Let's not make value judgments on others, though. Concentrate on what you can see. Really look. Squint if you have to."

Shadows, I thought. Someone yelled, "Shadows."

"Good."

Lines, spaces, shapes, contrast, rough surfaces, smooth surfaces, cold. "Holland," Mackel called my name.

I flinched.

"What do you see?"

"Um . . ." I gulped a grapefruit, then voiced my observations.

He clicked to the next slide. Was I right? I caught Cece peering back at me and smiling. Guess so.

We continued this exercise for another fifteen minutes until Mackel ran out of slides or we ran out of enthusiasm. As the lights came back on, he said, "We're going to repeat last week's assignment. My fault for not giving you more direction. I haven't taught Drawing I in a few years, as you can probably tell.

"Again, choose a single object in the room to sketch. Focus on the form. Examine the object carefully, more closely than you've ever looked at anything before. Feel free to wander around and get inspired. I'll play some music. Hopefully it'll stir the creative juices." He set a boom box on the stool and punched a button. Classical music streamed out.

It was soothing. I never listened to classical. Seth called it snooze muse. He hated country, too.

Okay, pick something. A chair, the door, a pottery vase on the shelf. Not very intriguing. I scanned the room a few more times. The only thing my focus kept returning to was the back of her head. There was texture there. Form, movement, interest. I flipped open my sketchbook and began to draw.

▼▲▼

She was waiting for me in the hall after class. Great. Motioning her to an enclave by the drinking fountain, I said, "They rejected it."

"No." She slapped her chest. "What a surprise." Looking off into the distance, she narrowed her eyes and said, "This place makes me sick. I really hate it here. It's like all the homophobes were exiled to this school."

"No they weren't." There might be a couple.

"Nobody's even out here. Haven't you ever wondered why?" Cece's eyes met mine.

"I, I guess I didn't think we had any gays."

She let out a short laugh. "Holland, open your eyes."

I did, and only saw her.

She shook her head. "What was their reason for *rejecting* us?"

"They didn't reject *you*. Mr. Olander said it wasn't inclusive enough. Official clubs need to be open to all the students." I pulled out the form. "Maybe you could add —"

"Straights." Cece's head bobbed. "A Gay/Straight Alliance, right? Gee, I'll have to up the membership to sixteen." She snatched the app from my hand. "Sorry. We don't want a GSA. At least, I don't. Straights don't understand what we're about, what we're going through. We can't talk about stuff that really matters, like coming out. Like dealing with harassment. Like sex."

My mouth went suddenly dry. "Okay. That makes sense. I'll try again." I reached for the application.

"I don't want to hassle you," she said.

"Cece, don't."

She ripped the form in half. The bell rang and she took off.

"Cece," I called after her. She started running. I chased her to the stairwell, then lost her. Slumping against the railing, I closed my eyes and fought off the static in my head. "It's no hassle," I murmured over the internal din. "I'd fight for you."

▼▲▼

There was a charge in the air that afternoon, people whispering. I caught a snatch of conversation behind me before econ class started, my ears pricking up at the words, "Gay club."

67

I whipped my head around and saw one girl stick a finger down her throat.

So that was it. News travels fast, I thought. And I bet I knew who was fueling the rumor mill.

"Holland. Oh, good." Kirsten rushed up behind me after school. I was headed for swim team practice. "I need to talk to you," she said.

I whirled on her. "Why are you telling people about the lesbi-gay club? What we talk about in student council is private."

She drew back. "I know that. I haven't said anything."

She looked offended, and sounded it. "Listen, Trevor and I were wondering if you and Seth wanted to go out with us on Friday night. Well, I was wondering." Kirsten swallowed hard. "We're always hanging out with Trevor's friends and they're so . . . I don't know. Boring. Haley Ackerson's parents are out of town and she's having this party Friday night. Will you come with us?"

"Um, sure. Okay." I felt off balance. Guilty for accusing her. "Friday? Oh, wait. I have a swim meet on Friday."

Kirsten's face darkened, like she thought I was lying.

"I do," I said.

"Okay, whatever. I just wanted you to spend more time with Trevor. Get to know him. He's really sweet, Holland. I know you'd like him if you just gave him a chance."

"I like him." That wasn't fair. That wasn't the issue.

Kirsten's eyes grazed the floor. "You think he's too young for me. I know that. But he's not. He's really mature for his age. He's the first guy I've ever met who doesn't just want to jump in the sack, you know? He cares about me. He loves me. He really

68

does." Kirsten sounded anxious, needy. Leah's words echoed in my head: She thinks you judge her.

"Maybe we could go Saturday night," I told her. "To a movie or something." I hated parties, anyway. They were just excuses for getting loaded and making out en masse.

Kirsten brightened. "Cool. Okay. We could go out to dinner or something first." She hugged me. "Thanks, Holland. I'm sorry about earlier," she said. "At the meeting. You know me, I live to play devil's advocate." Her eyes gleamed.

As she sauntered off, I stared at her back. Since when? The only side Kirsten ever took in a debate was her own. There were times I didn't get her. I didn't get her at all.

When I pushed through the door at the bottom of the stairs, I caught sight of Cece near the juice machine outside the locker rooms. She was standing with a couple of guys from the gymnastics team, I think. The door to the weight room was open. Something about the look on her face made me quicken my step.

As I got closer, one of the guys flattened his hand on the machine over Cece's head and said, "Come on, one kiss. Try it, you'll like it." He puckered his lips and made smooching sounds.

Cece stiffened. "Get away from me," she said. "What's your problem?"

"It's not *my* problem."

The other guy grabbed Cece's arm and shoved her against the machine. "Feel this? Huh?"

"Hey," I yelled, sprinting the rest of the way. Both guys whipped their heads around. "Leave her alone!" I wedged myself between them. "What the hell are you doing?"

The guys backed off. "Nothing. Just goofing around."

Cece bolted for the stairs.

"Cece, wait." I left the muscleheads in my dust.

She was halfway up the steps when I snagged her arm. I spun her around and said, "Are you okay?" She was shaking. God.

"Sick, Holland," she said. "You have sick people here."

"Not everyone. A couple of guys." I narrowed my eyes in their direction. "Jerks."

She shook her head and started up the steps again.

"Cece." I couldn't hold onto her. "We'll report them for sexual harassment."

She stopped at the top of the stairs and turned around. "No," she said. "No. It'll only make it worse."

"We can't just let them get away with it."

"Yes, we can." She swallowed hard. "They'll come after me." Her face paled and she let out a shudder. "Forget it." She ducked around me and charged out the east door.

"Hi, Holl." A couple of girls on swim team approached. "We better get our asses down there or Chiang'll make us do sprint sets again."

"Right." Her fear still pulsed through me. Blindly, I stumbled down the stairs.

Chapter 9

I didn't see her on Tuesday. She never materialized at her locker and wasn't in art. Jerks. I should've reported them myself. Her absence worried me. What if she never came back? What if I never saw her again? That night I leafed through the phone book to find "Goddard." There were dozens. Too many to call. What would I say, anyway? "Does Cece live here?" What if she did? What if she answered?

"Please," I'd say. "Don't leave. Come back and subject yourself to more violation and sexual assault."

God, what if she felt that way? What if she felt threatened? I was up all night obsessing about it. About her. I must've drifted off sometime because I woke up to Mom shaking my shoulder. "Holl? You're going to be late," she said. "Didn't your alarm go off?"

Shit. I'd forgotten to set it.

Arbuthnot paused in mid-sentence as I slithered into class fifteen minutes past the late bell. I *had* to sit in back, didn't I, so my ass would be visible grass. "You're late, Holland." She stopped me in my tracks.

Let us state the obvious. Turning around in the aisle, I smiled and said, "Sorry, Mrs. Arbuthnot. We had a family emergency this morning. My dad's going to live, though. The EMTs caught the heart attack in time."

That shut her up. Shut everyone up. To the people I passed on the way to my desk, I mouthed, Nooo. Shook my head. They smothered grins.

Arbuthnot mumbled an apology. As I slid into my seat, I noticed she seemed a little off kilter now. Good. Just doing my part to curb harassment at its source. "You'll, um, each prepare a character sketch of *Beowulf*," Arbuthnot said, sifting through a pile of books on her desk. She knocked one off. "Focus on what you believe are his most telling personality traits. Analyze how and why each is important to his development as a warrior."

The guy in front of me raised his hand.

"Yes, Marcus," Arbuthnot acknowledged, regaining composure.

"Can we pick the fact that Wulfie is gay?"

My spine fused. People twisted their heads to gawk at Marcus. They swiveled back to catch Arbuthnot's reaction. She said, "And how did you come to *that* conclusion?"

"The scene with him and his merry men, splashing around in the water. Seems pretty swishy to me." He waggled a limp wrist.

Everybody laughed.

Arbuthnot's face went purple. "Leave the room immediately," she snarled, pointing to the door.

"What? I'm just saying . . ."

"Out!" she shouted.

Marcus cursed under his breath, then scraped back his chair and shoveled his books into his arms. He strutted out, wiggling his hips all the way. The catcalls trailed him through the door.

Any other time I might've found him slightly amusing. Today I wanted to stand and scream, "What is this? National Gay Bashing Week?" But I couldn't. I couldn't command my muscles to move. Couldn't get out of my chair. Couldn't bring myself to do what I knew was right.

▼▲▼

She wasn't in art. She was gone forever, I knew it. When I got home after work, I felt sick. Physically ill. Mom asked at dinner if I was okay and I lied; said, "Yeah, fine." She was so busy fussing with Hannah, who was coming down with a cold and acting unusually cranky, that she didn't pursue it. Didn't push. Neal had been on the phone ever since we sat down to eat, hollering at his hard-of-hearing dad, which was giving me a headache to go along with my stomachache. I moved food around on my plate, then excused myself and trudged down to my room.

How many were there? I wondered. Four, a dozen, the whole school? When had it begun? Had Southglenn always been this way? So hostile? We had a strong policy against bullying, but how was that any different from harassment or discrimination? It was all about hate. There should be laws. Were there laws? Can you legislate against hatred? Why hadn't we discussed this in any of my government classes?

Cece's question burned in my brain: Why weren't more gays out? She seemed to imply, or know for sure, that we had more gays and lesbians in our school. Who were they? Where were they hiding? Did they walk the halls in fear of their lives? God, I couldn't imagine that. Every day, having to act invisible, protect yourself. Having to put up with assholes and bigots.

"Holland," Mom called down the stairs. "You have company."

Cece? Could it be?

I took the stairs two at a time and rushed into the living room. "Leah. Hi." Of course it wasn't Cece. She didn't know where I lived. Leah sat on the edge of the recliner, bouncing Hannah in her lap.

"I can't believe how big she is." Leah spread Hannah's arms apart and played pat-a-cake. "It's only been a few weeks since I've seen her, hasn't it?" she asked Mom, who was folding baby clothes next to Neal on the sofa. Some stupid reality show on TV had a fat guy fastening a bungee belt around his middle. "I was just here over Christmas," Leah said.

"They grow up fast." Mom smiled at me. "Too fast."

"No kidding," Leah said. "Her hair's gotten darker. Plus, she's put on like twenty pounds."

"Ten of that is the dump in her diapers." I fanned the air. "Whew, Hannie. A little too much mashed banana."

Mom tossed me a Huggies.

"I'll do it." Leah held out a hand and I passed her the diaper. I'd known Leah practically my whole life and could tell something was up. She wasn't crazy about babies, since she had three bratty little brothers. She rarely dropped by in the evening when we were in school. She worked and I worked, or I had practice, or I had Seth. A wave of guilt washed over me. I never had found time for a real heart-to-heart with Leah.

74

I was going to say, Bring Hannah to my room, but Leah laid her out on the rug to change her. The dryer buzzed downstairs. Mom slapped Neal's leg and said, "Come on, honey. Be a good role model and help me with the laundry."

"Now?" Neal whined. "But he's going to jump off the cliff."

"Holland will let you know if he lives." Mom scooped Hannah off the floor.

Thank you, I mouthed as she passed by. Neal traipsed after her, grumbling.

I curled cross-legged on the floor next to Leah. "What's up?"

She exhaled a long breath. "Conner broke up with me."

"Oh, my God," I gasped. I scrabbled to my knees and threw my arms around Leah, expecting her to disintegrate in tears, suffer an emotional meltdown, implode. She didn't. Didn't react at all. I drew back.

"It's not like I wasn't expecting it," she said.

"Were you?" This was news to me. "I thought you were deliriously happy." That's what she always said whenever anyone asked. "'We're deliriously happy. We couldn't be happier.'"

She fondled her ring finger, which was now empty. "Things were sort of weird over Christmas. Even before that, he hadn't been e-mailing me as often. Or calling. I think he really wanted to break up before Christmas, but he didn't have the heart."

"The balls, you mean." I shook my head. "God, Leah. You never told me there was anything wrong."

She met my eyes. "I was hoping it was just me. You know how I am. If anyone's even in a bad mood, I figure it's something I did or said."

I rubbed her arm. "What did he say exactly?"

75

"Exactly?" She tilted her head at an odd angle. "His exact words were, 'I'm setting you free.'"

Oh, no. That could only mean . . .

"Obviously he's met someone else." Leah's head dropped.

"Bastard. I never did like him."

Leah let out a short laugh. "That's what my mom said. Not that I told her first; she was just standing there when he called tonight. You're the first one I've told."

Whatever difference that made. "Your mom's right. The guy's a prick."

"Yesterday, he was God's gift. Today he's a prick."

"Leah —"

"It's okay. I understand." She scooped up a rubber ducky from the floor and squeezed it. "It's for the best, really. It never would've lasted. We don't have the same thing you and Seth do. The fire, you know? The passion." She smiled at me.

The passion. Right. Screams blasted from the TV and I remoted it off. "So, what are you going to do? Next year, I mean. You were so psyched about Americorps."

"Only because *he* was." Leah set the duck atop a box of baby wipes. "I don't know. Remember how you and me and Kirsten always talked about getting an apartment together after high school? Going to the same college? That was our dream."

Yeah, a hundred years ago. The apartment still sounded like fun.

"Kirs has been talking about Western State. Her cousin goes there and he really likes it. Maybe I'll apply with her." Leah pushed to her feet and wandered over to the picture window. Drawing the sheers, she gazed out into the night and added,

"Kirsten's going to shit a brick when she hears about Connor." Leah twisted her head around to look at me. "Maybe not. She was more in love with him than I was, I think."

"Kirsten was in love with his money," I muttered. "But then, so was I."

"So was I," Leah said. We both cracked up. She released the curtains and turned, folding her arms around herself. "It was nice to dress up and go out. All those society dances and fund-raisers his mother was involved in . . ."

"Don't forget the flowers and candy and crap."

"That too." Her eyes shone. The light extinguished when she added, "But sometimes he made me feel like he was buying me. Like, for instance, he always let me know exactly how much he'd spent, so I'd feel obligated to —" She stopped.

My jaw unhinged. "Have sex with him?"

"No," she said quickly. "No, it wasn't like that. He never forced me or anything. I probably just imagined it." She shook her head. "I'm mad at him, that's all."

"Leah, if you felt that way, it was real. You have every right to be pissed. Come on."

Her face changed. "You're right. Especially if he's been cheating on me."

"Oh, Leah." I wanted to hold her. Comfort her. I knew her well enough to know she was devastated. She'd made all these plans; rearranged her life around him. Before I could get up and go to her, she lowered herself to the sofa and bent over, elbows on knees. "What are you doing next year?" she asked. "Going to college with Seth, probably, huh? You couldn't talk him into Western State, could you?"

Mom bustled into the room. "You can't be serious," she said.

How long had she been standing there, listening? I hated when she did that.

Settling Hannah into her baby seat beside me, Mom said, "You girls need bigger dreams. There's no way Holland's going to a state school. I know Seth wouldn't dream of it. And you shouldn't either, Leah. It'd be a waste of your talent."

"Unless, of course, your talent is human waste," I murmered.

Mom looked at me. I looked at her back. How did she know what Seth dreamed of?

Leah said to me, "Have you decided? Seth was asking me yesterday if you'd said anything."

"Jesus." I shot to my feet. "Why doesn't everybody just get off my back." I stormed into the kitchen, almost colliding with Neal. We side-stepped each other, being careful not to touch. As I wrenched open the refrigerator and grabbed the milk carton, I sensed Leah behind me. She said, "I'm sorry, Holland. I didn't know it was a sore subject."

I took a slug of milk, set the carton back in the fridge, then plastered on my don't-worry-about-it smile. "I haven't decided, okay? Seth assumes I want to go with him, but I don't know what I want."

"Okay," Leah said. "No pressure."

No pressure. Right. So why was I on the verge of explosion?

"You want to come with me to tell Kirsten about Connor?" Leah said. "We shouldn't leave her out. You know how she gets."

I didn't really want to go. It was late, I didn't feel well. "Sure. Let me get my shoes." I padded over and gave Leah a hug. What are friends for?

78

Thursday Cece reappeared, huddling in front of her locker with her coffee and donuts and earphones, the baseball cap on her head. She wore a T-shirt that screamed: OUT! AND PROUD!

I was so glad to see her, the hall lights grew brighter.

Her eyes were closed, but she blinked up at my approach. Hi, I mouthed.

She removed the earphones. Leaning forward a little, she reached around and shut her locker door.

I dropped my duffel. "Oh, my God." Both hands rose to cover my mouth. "My God." Someone had spray-painted down the length of her locker: DIE DYKE.

"Not terribly artistic, were they?" Cece cocked her head upward. "I mean, the letters all run together. There's no style at all. Really amateurish. Not to mention extremely unoriginal."

I couldn't breathe. Couldn't speak. Didn't realize tears were streaming down my face until Cece shouted, "Don't!" She rushed across the hall and pinned me against my locker. "Don't cry. Don't you let them see us cry." Her eyes pooled with tears. She retreated and gathered her stuff.

I stood frozen, stunned. Her words echoed in my ears: Us? What did she mean by us? She was fleeing down the hall.

I gaped at her locker. How could they? Anger burbled up from my core. How *could* they?

I found out soon enough she wasn't the only one targeted. Brandi's locker had the same message, and three guys got the more obscene FAGS FUCK OFF.

It spurred a hurried assembly. Mr. Reynardi threatened the

entire student body with legal action for what he called "this delib-erate act of vandalism, this marring of school property, this crim-inal mischief."

Criminal mischief? He made it sound like a stupid prank. What about destruction of people's lives? What about destroying their trust in others?

Reynardi ranted on and on about prosecuting to the fullest ex-tent of the law, blah, blah, blah. He wanted names and he wanted them now.

Get real. Like someone's going to stand up and confess? Rat out their friends?

After the assembly I was so irate, I stormed to my locker. Cece was there. The others who'd been tagged were hanging out at her locker, too. One of the guys had a videocam and was shooting a tape of Cece, as if she were starring in a silent movie — making the discovery of the hateful message, tearing her hair out. She was funny. Made me want to laugh. I couldn't laugh. I felt too an-gry, too numb. I heard her ask for a copy of the tape because it'd make great PA.

What's PA? I wondered.

I was so intent on watching her — them — that I didn't notice the crowd forming. A dozen or so people had circled around and were closing in on Cece and the others. The guy with the video-cam lowered it slowly. There was this prolonged moment of si-lence, tension so thick you could taste it. Oh, my God, I thought. It's a lynch mob. They've come to finish the job. Say something, my brain commanded. Speak up.

"I wanted to say I'm sorry this happened to you," a voice carried in from the rear. I recognized it. "I hope you don't think we're all this way," Leah said.

There was a general murmur of agreement. Cece and the others didn't respond. Most of them cowered against the lockers, looking freaked. They looked to Cece for direction. She clapped once and said, "Okay, let's get this on film. You guys can be extras. I want to see moral outrage here, and fury. Like this." She shook a fist at the crowd to demonstrate. "Anyone got a beer? We could do foaming at the mouth."

Laughter filtered through the crowd.

Cece cued the camera, and the extras really got into it, hamming it up and acting out. Across the hall, Cece's eyes found mine. They spoke the truth; she wasn't enjoying this. She was humiliated. Hurt. Afraid. Her fear was so palpable it made my blood curdle. I wanted to find whoever had done this to her and kill them.

Chapter 10

"Did you finish your essays on those two applications?" Mom asked at dinner. "They have to go out next week."

"Yes," I said.

Mom eyed me. Cece was right, I was a terrible liar. "I'll do them tomorrow."

"You keep saying that." Mom passed the bowl of creamed corn to Neal. "You're running out of tomorrows."

Running out of tomorrows, I repeated to myself in my room, sprawling across my bed to begin another midnight marathon of homework. Sometimes I felt as if there were no tomorrows, that everything, my whole life, was crammed into one long day. A continuous stretch of meaningless time. Sometimes I even *wished* there was no tomorrow, if this was all I had to look forward to.

I opened my econ text, then shut it. I scrounged in my pack for my sketchbook instead. So far it included a full-page, cross-hatched drawing of Cece's head, a side shot of her ear, a drawing of her right hand on the art table with the assortment of rings she always wore. I wasn't close enough to get details of the patterns in the rings.

On the next page was a picture of the light switch — wow, that was exciting. I flipped to a blank page. With a half-moon shadow from my study lamp, the basement rafters would make a stunning still-life. Ugh. I needed inspiration. What was it Mackel said? "Let it come. Don't force it. Just free-draw." Which, to me, meant free fall. It was at times like this I wished I did drugs.

Okay. I got up and searched through my CDs. Didn't get too far. I cranked up the volume on Dixie Chicks and lay back, closing my eyes, to "let it come."

What came was her. The way one side of her mouth cricked up a little higher than the other when she smiled. That freckle, or mole, right above her lip. The sparkle in her eyes, the warmth. The fire, too, when she was pissed. Her skin, how it seemed to glow. I positioned my pencil and began to transfer the image of her from my mind to paper.

The CD ended and I focused on what I'd drawn. Her head, sporting a baseball cap, not a bad likeness. Her face was wrong, though. Out of symmetry. I could see her so clearly in my mind's eye, hear her laughing. That sound, the music in her voice.

The sensation was stirring. It aroused me in a way . . . almost as if . . .

As if I was falling for her.

Okay, that didn't shock me. I'd had crushes on girls before. I mean, who hadn't? I'd see a girl in the mall or at swim meets and think, Wow, would I ever like to meet *her*. I wouldn't act on the impulse or anything. I'd stop myself.

That's what it was with Cece. An innocent crush. I admired her. She was strong, self-confident. So damn cool. Attractive in a way only another girl would see.

What *did* I see? I didn't know exactly. Couldn't capture it on paper. It — she — wouldn't stay still.

I lay the sketchbook aside and scrambled to my feet, ejecting the CD and tossing it in my bag. At the top of the stairs, I ran into Mom and Neal in the kitchen, necking. "Ooh, caught ya," I said, waggling an accusatory finger.

Mom actually blushed. Removing my parka from the coat rack, I informed them, "I'm going out for a while."

"In this weather?" Mom looked aghast.

"I'm wearing clean underwear. Just in case."

▼▲▼

Washington Central was farther than it seemed. I'd printed out an Internet map at the computer lab during study hall today. The legend was misleading; it had to be more than twenty-five miles away, and the streets were sheer ice. A stoplight changed unexpectedly and I slammed on the brakes, skidding through the intersection. Horns blared and an SUV narrowly missed me.

Shit. My heart hammered against my ribs. What was I doing?

Had to see her. Talk to her. Apologize about the locker incident. About the assholes in our school. Try to make it right. Even though the janitors had painted over the lockers by the end of the day — covered up the crime so we could all pretend it never happened — she had to be freaked. I wanted to quell her fears.

Depressing the gas pedal slightly and swerving away from the curb, I inched along toward town. After circling the block a couple of times, I spotted it: Hott 'N Tott Donuts.

Ten minutes later I was still huddled in the parking lot, shivering from cold. Not only from the cold. "This is stupid," I muttered. "Get out already." What was I afraid of?

Her, that's what. This had nothing to do with the locker incident. I wanted her to like me. Wanted to find out if she did. Was that important enough to risk my life over? Apparently.

So cold. I started the engine again and cranked up the heater.

She wasn't even here. I hadn't caught a glimpse of her through the plate glass window in the year I'd been stalling, freezing my butt off. I was safe. Just came to check the place out, buy a cup of coffee. Reasonable, rational. Only one customer had braved the weather — a cab driver who was hunched over one of the tables, nursing a cup of coffee while thumbing through the newspaper.

"Just go get a donut. What's the big deal?"

Okay. I bolstered my courage. Opened the Jeep door and got out.

"Evenin'. Help ya?" the older man behind the counter asked. He smiled kindly. Was this Cece's uncle?

I smiled back. "I'll, um, have one of those." I pointed to a glazed cinnamon twist. "And . . . do you have hot chocolate?"

"Sure do. What size?"

I skimmed the cup display. "Medium, I guess."

"For here or to go?" He stoked up the cocoa machine.

My eyes searched the interior. No sign of her. "To go," I answered.

He finished my order and rang it up. "Is Cece here?" I asked, handing him a five.

"Cecile!" he shouted through a rear door.

"What?" she shouted back.

My heart raced. Exploded.

"You got company."

Cece appeared out of nowhere, wiping her floured hands on an apron. The top of her head was covered in a blue bandanna, tied gypsy style. When she saw me, she stopped dead in the doorway.

Well, finally, I'd managed to shock *her*. "Hey." I hitched my chin. "I was in the neighborhood."

The hint of a smile cricked her lips. "Unc, okay if she comes back?"

He eyed me up and down. "Sure, I guess." He opened the counter top, which was hinged on one side. "No funny business." He pointed at Cece.

She blew out a puff of air at him.

What did he mean by that? No funny business.

Cece walked across the room to a long butcher block table. I followed. "You can pull up a stool if you want," she said over her shoulder.

I set down my cocoa and twist on the table, then dragged over a high-backed stool and climbed aboard.

Cece lifted a rolling pin and ran it over a circle of dough. "What are you doing here really?" she asked.

"Like I said —"

"In the neighborhood." Her eyes cut to me and she grinned. "Let me just get these in the proofer. It'll only take a minute." She sprinkled cinnamon and sugar on the dough, rolled it into a snake, and sliced it into identically sized wedges, as if she'd been doing this all her life.

"I'm sorry about what happened today," I said.

"Forget it. It's not your fault. Grab me that pan." She pointed.

I flinched at her sudden movement. I pulled out a large, aluminum tray from the rack behind me and handed it to her. With a spatula, she flipped the wedges onto the tray, then carried it to a glassed-in case where racks of similar pans were resting. Proofing, I surmised. I'd never seen the inner workings of a donut shop. It was all shiny metal and spicy smells. Sparkling and sweet and warm. So why was I trembling?

Cece returned, exhaling a weary breath, and leaned against the cutting table, arms folded.

"What?" I said.

She smiled and shook her head at the floor. "Nothing."

"You work here every night?" I sipped my cocoa.

"Why don't you drop by and find out." She lifted her eyes and held mine.

Two could play at this game. "You'd like that, wouldn't you?"

She set down the spatula. "What do you think?" she said.

I think I couldn't breathe.

"Cecile, when you're done with the rolls would you mix a batch of egg batter for the morning?" her uncle called through the door.

"Slave driver," she called back.

I liked that, the banter. I liked everything about her.

"What?" She zeroed in on me again.

I blinked away, realizing I'd been staring at her. "I don't know." My eyes skimmed the floor tiles. Checkerboard.

"If you don't know, then I can't help you." Cece moved past me, almost grazing my arm. Almost.

"Okay, so I'll just help myself," I quipped, retrieving my cinnamon twist off the table and chomping off the end.

She disappeared into a back room. A few seconds later she stepped out, lugging a bag of flour. "Look," she said, dumping the bag on the table. "I really have a lot to do, okay? And I don't like playing games."

Heat fried my face. "I'm sorry." I slid off the stool; stumbled. Dropped my twist on the floor. "I'll go." I picked it up. As I staggered for the open doorway to flee, escape, I heard her curse and pound the table with a fist.

She hates me, I thought. What have I done? Oh, God. She hates me.

▼▲▼

For the first time in my life, I didn't get all my homework finished. I set my alarm for five A.M., but instead of hitting the books, I went swimming.

The lights were still off in the pool area when I got there and it was so quiet my bare feet echoed. I dove in.

The cold surged through my veins — a welcome relief. I concentrated on my muscles contracting, my arms slicing through the water. Soon the rhythm of my breathing and stroking and breathing and stroking drowned out my thoughts. Banished my feelings to a dark recess in my mind, where they should be banished.

Forget her. Force her out of your head, get her out of you.

I don't know how long I swam, lap after lap after mind-numbing lap. My lungs and muscles collapsed simultaneously, and I let my final kick propel me to the edge.

Where she was sitting, elbows on knees. She looked me in the eye and said, "I was in the neighborhood."

Chapter 11

I wrenched off the shower faucets, but wasn't about to go gallivanting through the locker room half naked. Although . . .

She likes me. I smiled to myself. I wonder what she'd do if —

My phone rang. Before I could think, Cece called, "I'll get it."

Toweling my head, I heard her say, "Who? No, sorry. What number did you dial?"

I gave my prickled body a once over and wrapped the towel around me. A little lower than usual. Grabbing my wet swimsuit off the floor, I padded to the benches, asking, "Who was it? My mother?"

"Wrong number." Cece scanned me up and down, then let out a breath. She stood abruptly and said, "I need coffee. Gotta fly."

I sank to the bench, feeling embarrassed, exposed. Stupid. I quickly dressed.

▼▲▼

On the way to my Jeep at lunch to head for McDonald's, Kirsten said, "Oh, by the way, Holland, Seth. Saturday night's off. Trevor dumped me."

I skidded to a stop on the icy parking lot. "Kirsten, oh no. What happened?"

"The funniest thing. His mother doesn't approve of me. Says I'm too old for her little Trevie. I guess word got back to her that I was a slut." Her glare sliced through me.

What? I never — "Oh, excuse me," she added. "A player."

"Kirsten," I protested, then said more gently, "I'm really sorry." I was. She looked miserable. She wasn't even wearing makeup today, her face was all pale and blotchy.

She gazed off into the distance. "I can never keep anything good." Her eyes pooled with tears. I reached to hug her, but she climbed into the back of the Jeep, scooting over to the far side and staring straight ahead.

Leah and I exchanged glances. I think Leah already knew. She crawled in beside Kirsten and patted her knee. Felt her pain, I suppose, more than me.

"Saturday night?" Seth said at my side. "What was Saturday night?"

Oops. Guess I forgot to tell him. "Nothing. Doesn't matter now." He was going to say something else, but I cut him off by handing him the keys. "You drive." Normally Seth rode shotgun, but today he'd brought along Coop, so I figured he'd appreciate the opportunity to amp up the testosterone.

McD's was jammed with little kids squealing and chasing each other around Playland. As the five of us claimed a booth in back,

I said to Kirsten, "Do you want me to come over tonight? Talk about it?"

"No. I'm all right. He's a momma's boy. So what? He was getting on my nerves, anyway." She stuck a straw through the lid of her diet Coke. "So is your lezzie friend going to reapply for a Gay Straight Alliance?" she asked.

"No," I answered, a slow burn spreading through my gut. "Don't call her that, okay? Her name is Cece." I lifted my Big Mac to my mouth. "She doesn't want a GSA. Just a gay club." I took a bite.

"See?" Kirsten bent over to sip her soda. "Agenda."

I chewed and swallowed fast. "There is no gay agenda." I tried to control my voice, my temper.

"Could I have some ketchup?" Leah interrupted.

Around in front of me, Seth passed her a handful of packets.

Kirsten said, "Did you see the shirt she was wearing yesterday? That OUT! AND PROUD!?" She curled a lip.

"What's wrong with it?" I said.

Kirsten shook her head. "She's just so obvious. Look at me, I'm gay. I'm special," she mocked.

My jaw clenched. I set down my burger, deliberately.

Leah piped up, "I don't think that's what she's doing. She's just being who she is."

I sent Leah a silent thank you.

Leah added, "I imagine it's pretty lonely being the only out person in school. I think she's incredibly brave. I don't know how they find each other if they're not out."

Coop said, "They list their phone numbers in the john. 'For a good time, call Bruce. 1-800-222 —'"

Kirsten snorted. Coop smirked. He said, "You know what gay means, don't you? Got AIDS Yet?"

Seth pre-empted my explosion. "Shut up, Coop. That isn't funny. You going to eat that?" He indicated my Big Mac.

I shoved it over to him.

Kirsten dipped a Chicken McNugget into a cup of barbecue sauce and popped it into her mouth. "She's just trolling for meat," she said with her mouth full. Turning to Coop, she added, "And not the Oscar Mayer weiner variety."

He choked on a fry.

That did it. I elbowed Seth. "Let me out."

"What? We're not done."

"I am."

He just sat there.

"Move!"

Seth scooted off the end of the bench. I pushed past him and stormed out the exit.

I hated how they talked about them. About her. Kirsten, Coop, all of them. Especially Kirsten. I understood that she hurt, she was venting, directing her pain elsewhere. Still, she should just shut up.

We drove back in silence. At least, I did. Coop apologized, like that was going to make it all better. Seth tried to tickle me once and I slugged him. I was still fuming when I got to art. I kicked a chair and sent it crashing into the easel up front.

My brain engaged. Chill, Holland. God.

On impulse I took the chair next to the window and waited for Cece to arrive. Needed to feel her presence, her strength.

Needed to protect her from all the ugliness in the world. As I dug in my pack for my sketchbook, a body descended on me. I glanced up.

"That's my seat," Brandi said.

"Do you mind if we switch? I'm having a hard time seeing the slides from the back." I nudged my glasses up the bridge of my nose.

She hesitated a moment, then wandered away. A few seconds later Cece sauntered in. She spotted me and held my eyes as she moved across the room. Floated. The chair next to me scraped back and a flash of orange hair caught my eye. "Yo," Winslow said in my ear.

"Winslow, I'm saving this —"

"Sorry I'm late." Mackel charged into the room. "Let's get started. We have a lot to cover today. You'll need your larger tablet for this exercise. And your marking pens."

Cece vanished. I twisted around to see she'd taken the empty seat in back next to Brandi. Shit.

▼▲▼

Faith was getting reamed out in her room when I got home from school. What was she doing here? I wondered. She'd stayed over *last* weekend. What happened to every *other* weekend? At the bottom of the stairs, I heard Mom snarl, "It's sacrilegious and I won't have it in my house. Grow up, Faith."

"You grow up!" Faith screamed at Mom. "Stay out of my stuff. Just get the hell out of my life. You're not my mother and you never will be."

I purposefully tripped over the laundry basket.

"Wait until your father hears about this," Mom said in a lowered voice.

Faith countered, "He won't care and you know it."

Mom charged across the basement, eyes flaming. "Hello, honey," she intoned between clenched teeth. "And how was *your* day?"

"About like yours."

She stomped up the stairs. As I rounded the partition, Faith said, "Bitch."

"Same to you," I replied.

"Not you. Her." She jutted her chin toward the ceiling. Rolling over on her bed, she scrunched in a fetal position and drew a pillow into her face. That's when I saw what Mom had gone ballistic over. Standing in the middle of Faith's dresser was a statue of the Virgin Mary clutching this headless baby Jesus. Sick.

Thank God I had a swim meet and wouldn't have to suffer through dinner with the AntiChrist and the Cleavers. As I was jamming a clean Speedo into my duffel, my phone rang. "What time do you think you'll be here?" Seth asked.

"Be where?"

He didn't speak for a long moment. "The apartment? This is Friday night."

It'd totally slipped my mind. "Seth, I have a swim meet."

"I know," he said. "When will you be back?"

I exhaled an irritated breath. "Just a sec." I retrieved my schedule that was pushpinned to the partition. "It's at Eagle Ridge, so probably ten, ten-thirty."

"Okay. What did you tell your mom about tonight?"

My mom? Crap. "Nothing yet."

"Holland," Seth's voice rose, "she'll have the National Guard out looking for you when you don't come home."

"Don't worry about it," I snapped. "I'll take care of it."

Seth's voice softened. "I'm sorry. I'm sorry about today, too. Coop's an idiot sometimes. I know you're upset about everything that's happened this week. So am I. We can discuss it tonight."

Discuss it. How "Seth." How would "discussing" it change anything? The world was full of hate.

"I love you," he said. And waited.

I wondered how long he'd wait. Forever, probably. The static in my head intensified. Finally, I couldn't bear the noise. "I love you, too."

Upstairs, I found Mom sitting at the credenza in the dining room, paying bills, her mini radio tuned to a talk show. With my hand on the doorknob, I called to her, "I'm going to my meet. See you tomorrow."

She craned her neck around the wall to peer at me. "Tomorrow?"

I opened the door. "I'm staying at Leah's tonight, remember? I'm sure I told you."

"I'm sure you didn't."

Damn. "It's all right, isn't it?"

"Leah's huh?" Mom licked an envelope and sealed it shut. "I don't expect you'll be there when I call later, will you?"

I blanched. "No."

"You are taking your pills, aren't you?"

I turned my burning face away.

"Holland?"

What business was it —

"Look, I'm not coming down on you. I understand about being young, being in love. I was there once, remember? I just want you to be careful. Don't do anything stupid that might jeopardize your future."

Like having a child you never wanted? I translated to myself. "I'm careful," I muttered.

Mom said, "Good luck at your meet."

I mumbled thanks and slithered out of there.

▼▲▼

All the way to Eagle Ridge I listened to the Dixie Chicks. Over and over. I'd memorized the lyrics already. Memorized her, too. Her face, her mannerisms, her smile. God, I loved her smile. I closed my eyes and let the music lift me up, sweep me away. Take me to another place, another time.

As we filed into the pool area to start the meet, my eyes combed the audience. Hoping, hoping . . . There. A baseball cap. Was that her against the bricks, staring at me? She was too far away to identify positively without my contacts, which I'd forgotten in my haste to get out of the house.

Coach Chiang gathered us together for a pep talk. Go Starfish.

I looked up again, but she was gone. If that was her, she never returned.

▼▲▼

Seth met me at the apartment door, a quart of Bud in his hand and a dishtowel over his arm. "Entréz, mademoiselle." He gestured me inside. In the living room, he'd built a fire in the fireplace, piled all the dirty clothes and trash into a heap, and cleared off the coffee table. Two placemats were set out with silverware and napkins. "Wow," was all I could say. Seth usually scored a low one-digit on the romance scale. "Is this for me?"

"No, it's for Kirsten. She's coming by later."

I smacked his chest.

"May I take your coat, Mademoiselle?" He extended an arm.

I loaded him down with my duffel and coat and backpack, which he dumped on the heap. "Dinner's in the oven," he informed me, handing me the bottle of beer. "Do the honors?"

"Of unscrewing the cap?"

He bowed again. "S'il vous plait."

Oh, brother.

"I shall return," he said, pivoting and scuttling off toward the kitchen like a sand crab.

What a goon. I swigged on the Bud as I trundled into the living room. Seth's brother and his roommates were slobs. I removed a crumpled Twinkies wrapper from the couch and sat. Guzzled the beer. A moment later Seth reappeared with two plates of Chinese food. It smelled fantastic. I was famished. He pulled out two wine glasses from his back pockets and set them on the coffee table. Oops. Guess he had bigger plans for the beer.

We shared one order of cashew chicken and a sweet-and-sour pork, plus four egg rolls and a vat of rice. Wiping my greasy fingers on a napkin, I said, "What's the occasion?"

"No occasion." Seth lifted his wine glass of sparkling Bud to toast. "Just us."

I clinked my glass against his. As we drank, I studied Seth's face. It was so familiar to me, every blemish, every line. The scar above his right eyebrow where he'd been whacked with a hockey stick. I felt as if I'd known him all my life, which was practically true. We'd gone to school together since elementary. It was Kirsten who'd set us up. She was dating his brother at the time, during her "older man" period, as opposed to her current "prepubescent" phase. I'd never even considered going out with Seth. But it worked. It was good between us. Comfortable.

Maybe that was the problem. This attraction to Cece, this crush or whatever it was, was exciting, new, unpredictable. I didn't know where it would lead, or even where I wanted it to lead. I think I knew where it *could* lead.

And if it did . . .

"Where are you?" Seth's voice jerked me back to reality.

"I'm here." I smiled at him. "With you."

He tossed a couple of sofa pillows onto the hearth and crooked his finger at me. I slid off the couch. We nuzzled together by the fire. Seth started to kiss me. After a while, he whispered, "Let's take this to the bedroom."

"You know what? I'm really tired." I yawned and stretched.

"What?" He drew away from me. "I set all this up for you. For us. What's the matter?"

The way he was looking at me — so angry, hurt. I couldn't hurt him. "Nothing." I shook my head at the floor. "Come on."

▼▲▼

I slipped out from under the sheet, trying not to breathe.

"Holl?" Seth turned over. "Where you going?"

"Home. Sorry. Go back to sleep." I pulled on my sweatpants.

"But we have all night." He pushed to his elbows.

"I know. I can't." My voice sounded hoarse, hollow. "I don't feel good. I'm sorry." I lurched for the door. I needed to get out, get away. As far away from here as possible.

She was in me, in my blood, invading every cell in my body. She was the one I wanted. She was the one I saw, felt, desired. This was wrong. He was wrong. It was all so wrong.

Chapter 12

Saturday morning I woke to the bang of the washing machine lid. I staggered into the laundry room to find Mom sorting piles of clothes. "Mom?"

She jumped. "Holland, you're home. I didn't expect to see you until later." She tossed a pair of Neal's boxer shorts onto a pile of whites. "What happened? Did you and Seth have a fight?"

"No." I wish we had. It'd be easier. "I just wanted to come home."

A sudden chill made me shiver and I hugged myself. Mom came over and smoothed my messy hair. It'd been a rough night. "I'm glad." She smiled. "You sure you're okay? You look tired."

"I'm fine."

She followed me to my room. Faith, I noticed, was a lump under her bedspread. I found my glasses and put them on. "What time is it?" I glanced at the clock. "Six-thirty?" As in A.M.? No wonder I felt drugged. What was she doing starting the laundry at six-thirty? Talk about Supermom.

Supermom said, "Since you're home, how 'bout taking care of these college applications?" She slapped the stack of forgotten forms on my dresser.

I sighed wearily. "Oh. Okay." I'd never get back to sleep now, anyway.

"You could've been finishing these instead of whatever that is." She pointed to my tablet, which was open at the bottom of my bed. Had I left it open? "Why in the world are you taking art? What a waste of time."

I bristled. Wished her gone, and got my wish when the dryer buzzed.

It was a half-hearted effort, but I slogged through all the college apps and sealed them in their respective envelopes. Cornell, Stanford, Antioch. Talk about a waste of time. Even if they accepted me, I wasn't sure I'd go. Where was Antioch, anyway? I heard Faith roust herself and drag into the bathroom. When she came out, our eyes met briefly. She might've grunted. Her black mascara had tracked to her chin. Scary.

She clomped across the basement and up the stairs. She usually zoned in front of the TV on Saturday mornings, watching cartoons. That was about her speed.

I took a shower, then toasted a couple of Pop-Tarts and returned to my room to veg. To think. About him — not him. Her. Me. Her and me.

Stop it. Stop thinking. My eyes strayed to the dresser, where *Beowulf* beckoned. I retrieved the book and paged through to find the section about swimming with his merry men. Reread it. Pretty suggestive, all right. Made me remember all those times in swim team practice with the girls when we'd goof around, dunk each other, play chicken. Times I'd have to rein myself in because it was getting so intense.

I lowered the book to my lap. There were other times, too. Ms. Fielding, in German class. I was so in love with her. I used to pretend I needed help so I could stay after school. She wasn't gay, I don't think. Just beautiful. And Leah. God. I had a torrid crush on Leah in sixth grade. Seventh grade. Eighth grade . . .

My pulse quickened. Was I? Gay, I mean? If so, what was I doing with Seth?

Maybe I was bi. That would explain it. An open heart, willing to give and accept love wherever it came from. The feelings, the stirrings, the awakening senses with Cece, though, I'd never experienced those with Seth. With any guy.

A crash against the wall made me leap off the bed. I charged around the partition between Faith's and my space. Fixed my gaze on the Virgin Mary that lay in shards by the laundry room, then Faith's smoldering glare. Mom yelled down the stairs, "This is *my* house and you'll obey *my* rules."

Faith locked eyes with me. She opened her mouth, then thought better of it, I guess, and flung herself backward on the bed, crossing her arms. A wave of sympathy washed over me. Faith wasn't having much luck with mothers. I'd only ever seen her real mom once when she dropped Faith off for the weekend, but I'd overheard a private conversation between Mom and Neal. He said his ex-wife was a workaholic, that she left Faith alone too much. He worried she was unsupervised. He'd like her to move in here permanently.

Mom nixed that idea, thank God. I should ask Faith about her mother, I thought. She was obviously suppressing a lot of anger. Sure, and I should major in psychology at Antioch. Maybe if we talked, though . . .

Faith cranked up her death rock and slapped on her earphones. Guess not. My phone rang.

I returned to my space and answered, " 'Lo?"

"Hey, babe."

My heart sank. "Hey."

Seth said, "Can I come over?"

"No. My mom's home." I cupped a hand around my mouth to muffle the sound. "And my wicked stepsister's here, too."

He clucked. "I didn't mean for that. You have a one track mind. Are you feeling okay?"

"Yeah," I lied.

"We won't do Chinese again. That stuff's lethal; I'm still burping cabbage. We need to get together about this leadership conference soon. I was hoping we could start today."

"Why did you get me involved in that, anyway? You know I'm up to my ass in work."

"If you don't want to do it, I'll find someone else."

"Good," I said. "Do that."

He hesitated. "Wrong answer."

I squeezed my eyes shut. This wasn't his fault. It wasn't about the conference.

"I just thought we'd have fun working together," he said. "Doing something besides . . . you-know-what. Isn't that what you wanted?"

I exhaled a long breath. "Maybe tomorrow I can find time."

"Find time? For me, you mean?"

I didn't reply.

He hung up.

Great. I considered calling him back, but the thought was fleeting. I didn't have the energy, or the motivation. Maybe I wanted him mad at me.

I opened my calc book and paged forward to chapter six — Monday's assignment. The numbers ran off the page. I was off the page. I needed to get out of here for a while.

I changed into a clean long-sleeved tee and a pair of drawstring pants, then pocketed my billfold. I'd driven halfway across town before I realized where I was going. Yeah, a donut would taste good, but there were about a dozen Dunkin' Donuts on my side of town.

Who was I kidding? I needed to see her. I didn't even know if she worked Saturdays. Didn't have a plan.

At Hott 'N Tott, I vanquished my fear à la Beowulf and boldly set forth. As I hopped up onto the curb, my eyes scanned the interior of the shop through the window, where I saw Cece sprawled lengthwise across one of the plasti-form benches, one knee clutched to her chest. My heart skipped a beat. She was wearing her gypsy scarf again, laughing at something the person across the table from her had said. The person made a wild hand gesture and Cece threw back her head and howled.

I pedaled backward, away from the door. My butt hit the hood of my Jeep and inched its attached human remains around to the driver's side. I reached for the handle, hoping, praying she hadn't seen me. As I pealed out, my tires spitting salt and sand, the person with Cece twisted her head to look out the window. I didn't have to see her face to know it was Brandi.

▼▲▼

That night I had a dream. An erotic dream. There was me in the pool, nude, and ahead of me another swimmer, just out of reach. I lengthened my strokes to catch up. Grabbed an ankle and pulled myself alongside. She turned and smiled. Cece. She was naked too, and instinctively our bodies came together. Our legs intertwined.

I woke with a start, breathing hard, wishing I could get it back. Get her back. Finish the dream. Find out how far it would go and what was waiting for me on the other side.

▼▲▼

Cece didn't show up at the pool on Monday. Not that I expected her to — hell, I don't know what I expected. Upstairs, wrenching open my locker, I glanced in my mirror to see her just arriving, setting her breakfast down in front of her locker. She caught my eye and smiled.

That smile.

"Holl!" Seth's voice whipped my head around. "Sorry I didn't make it over yesterday. My dad needed help fixing the garage door after Mom backed into it — again. Then Coop dropped by to work on this physics project." He loped up beside me. "You feeling better?"

I remembered, with a hopeless sigh, that Seth never could stay mad.

"What about we do it at lunch today since Olander's out and there's no student council meeting this week?"

"Do what?" I asked.

"The leadership conference?" He knuckled my head. "Olander's going to want to know where we are on it by next Monday." He caught a drip of water under my ear from my sopping wet hair. Guess I'd forgotten to towel it.

I gathered books. "Yeah, okay."

Seth lifted my chin and inclined his head. "I love you," he said.

Don't, I thought. Stop. Just stop loving me.

"Holland?" His eyes bore into mine.

I couldn't do it. Couldn't. "Yeah. Me, too." I forced a smile.

I let him kiss me, which he took advantage of and began to french. I wrestled away from him. "Seth."

He grinned and touched the tip of my nose. "See you later." He swaggered off.

I shouldered my bag and shut the locker.

"Do you love him?"

I jumped out of my skin. She was standing right beside me. "Who?"

Her eyes widened.

"Seth?" I peered over my shoulder at his retreating back. "Um, we've been going together for a long time. A year."

"That's not what I asked."

I couldn't look at her. Couldn't risk her seeing through me, reading me.

"Do you hear bells?" she asked.

I had to smile at that. "Bells?"

"You know, bells. Music, fireworks." She wiggled her eyebrows.

106

I let out a short laugh. It sounded strangled, same way I felt. "Only in my dreams."

"Oh, yeah?" She arched an eyebrow.

Why did I say that? God.

Cece said softly, "Maybe you should listen to your dreams."

My stomach suffered a major eruption.

She pushed off the locker she'd been balancing against with the sole of her shoe and said, "Think about it."

Like I haven't been. "Do you think about it?" I asked at her back.

She stopped and turned around. "I don't have to. I know."

Stampeding hooves interrupted our conversation as the entire track team thundered down the hall between us. By the time I elbowed through the bodies, she was gone.

▼▲▼

I agreed with everything Seth suggested for the leadership conference. Whether we set up the tables in a U or an open square made no difference to me. It was trivial. I wanted it gone. Wanted him gone.

"We didn't talk about how to split the participants up into corporations." Seth trailed me out the door of the media center. "Or who we want to invite as speakers for the panel."

"Whatever. You decide." Just go, I screamed silently. Let me go.

"How about after school? We could meet —"

"I have to work."

"Then tonight."

"Leah and Kirsten are coming over. They're both going through these major traumas, you know. I promised we'd get together." I was such a liar. Thank God he couldn't read me like Cece.

The late bell rang. "There's a teacher in-service on Wednesday," Seth called at my back. "We have the day off. Want to get together then?"

"Sure," I tossed over my shoulder.

"Ten o'clock. Come over to my house."

It barely registered. I sprinted down the arts wing. She was there, in class, talking and laughing with Brandi.

Brandi. I wished her gone, too. Cece and I made the briefest eye contact before I stumbled to my seat. Dazed, unsteady. My heart carved a cavern in my chest. All period long I tried to send Cece mental messages: Look at me, smile at me, be with me. Mackel gave us an assignment to draw the other half of a face. A child's face, from a picture he'd blown up. It forced me to focus my energy. Good. Concentrate on the face. The child. The task at hand.

I got so absorbed in the project, the period ended and chairs scraped back. Cece stood with Brandi. I ripped the page out of my tablet and rushed to the front of the room to hand in my assignment, to catch her, talk to her.

Mackel snagged my drawing off the top of the stack. "Whoa, whoa. Come back here, lady." He flagged me down. "Let's have a look at this."

Damn. Cece exited with Brandi. She glanced over her shoulder at me and held my eyes.

"Ooh, ooh," Mackel cooed over my drawing. "Tell me how you approached this."

"Um," I twisted back, "Head on. I really have to go." I shuffled backward toward the door.

"In. Credible." Mackel shook his head. "I can't even tell which of the halves you drew."

I raced out the door, sprinted to the stairwell, and skidded to a stop. No sign of her. Not in the halls, not on the stairs. Where could she be?

I thought I spotted her on my way to econ, then after class at the drinking fountain, then lurking outside the door to the gym, but each time I backtracked, she'd vanished. As if she was a mirage. Or an illusion. That was it, an illusion. Like my life — a reality just out of reach.

▾▲▾

My phone rang on the way to work. I dug through my bag on the seat beside me, cursing. I was already late, having stalled around to catch Cece at her locker and missing her again. Where was she? "Yeah, hello?" I snarled.

"Hi. Know who this is?"

My breath caught. "Cece, hi. I tried to find you all day. I wanted to finish our conversation."

"What conversation?" she said.

Didn't she even remember? The Conversation. About dreams, and bells, and music.

"Look, um, what I'm calling about . . ." She laughed a little. Nervous like. "Um, okay, if you're not doing anything tomorrow night, which you are, probably, with Seth, but I was wondering . . . do you like PA?"

Someone swerved in front of me and I slammed on the brakes. "Asshole," I hissed.

"Okay, forget it."

"Cece, no. Not you. God. I'm driving and some jerkoff just about ran me off the road. I love PA."

She laughed. "You're even a bad liar on the phone."

I had to chuckle. "Okay, what is it?"

"Performance art."

"Oh." Silence, crackle on the line. "Sorry," I said. "I still don't know what it is."

"It's kind of hard to explain," she said. "Everyone has their own interpretation, which is what makes it so awesome. Mostly it's expression. Physical and emotional expression, but it uses all the senses. It's really sensual. You'd like it."

A thrill shot through me. "Yeah, it sounds cool. So . . . tomorrow night?"

"There's a performance at the Rogue Theater. A bunch of PA groups from around the city. We got in at the last minute. Our group, I mean."

"You're in a group? You're a performer?"

"Uh huh. Would you like to come? I could get you a couple of free tickets."

A horn honked behind me and I realized I'd been stopped at a green light, holding up traffic. I burned rubber. "Sounds great," I told her. "I'd love to go. Not lying, am I?"

She laughed. I loved her laugh. "Are you on your way to Children's Cottage?" she asked.

"Yeah."

"Is it a fun job?"

I started to answer when someone hollered her name in the background. A man's voice, deep. "Gotta fly," she said quickly. "I'll bring your tickets tomorrow." The connection between us died.

How did she know where I worked? And how did she get my phone number? I pressed *69 to retrieve hers, scrambling in my bag for a pen and paper, and almost wiping out a city bus in the lane next to me.

Chapter 13

Miss Holland, Miss Holland, do me!" Courtney bounced up and down, flapping a page of newsprint in front of my face.

"You're next," I told her. "Let me finish Kevin." I studied his chubby face across the drawing table, so angelic, but with that devilish twinkle in his eye. The mouth wasn't quite right; the upper lip was crooked.

"Miss Holland. Miss Holland."

Judy placed a hand on my shoulder. "You have a line forming," she said.

I glanced over at Courtney, then behind her, where a bunch of kids were clutching pages of blank newsprint as fast as Mrs. Ruiz could tear them from a tablet.

"This is really good, Holland," Judy said, examining my drawing. "I never knew you were an artist."

"Neither did I," I admitted.

"Lemme see." Kevin grabbed the sheet from under my pencil lead and held it in front of his face. Lowered it. His eyes grew wide as waffles. "Aw, sweet!" he cried.

It made me laugh. Made Judy laugh, too. "Next victim," I called.

▼▲▼

Mom was in the basement ironing when I floated down the stairs. I lifted Hannah from her baby seat and tossed her into the air. She squealed. Mom scowled at me. Uh-oh.

"Look at this," she growled, holding up one of Faith's black T-shirts. DANTE was emblazoned on the front between licks of fire. On the back it read:

There is no light save from that perfect peace
Which never is clouded: it is else darkness,
Shadow of the flesh, or poison of its disease.
(Paradiso)

Mom asked, "What does that mean?"

"I have no idea," I said.

"It sounds obscene." She balled up the tee and dumped it in the trash. "I wish you'd talk to her, Holland. Tell her how ridiculous she looks. Get her off this Goth kick. It's not normal."

"I can't. We don't inhabit the same planet."

Mom shook her head. "I can't imagine what people think of her. Don't they make fun of her at school?"

"Not really." Because we have that anti-bullying policy that fosters peace and love in our hearts.

Mom went on, "She looks like a character out of a B movie, with all that makeup and those clothes."

113

I huffed a little. "No, she doesn't. She's just expressing herself. It's a free country." Don't ask me why I was defending Faith.

"Neal's embarrassed to even take her to his parents' house anymore. He thinks his dad'll have a stroke if Faith walks in there dressed like the grim reaper."

It was time to change the subject. "Can I throw my suit in the dryer?" I set Hannah down in her seat and removed two clammy Speedos from my duffel, along with the damp towel they were wrapped in. Tossed everything in the machine, then lifted the baby seat and lugged it to my room.

Mom appeared a few minutes later. She stacked a pile of clean clothes at the foot of my bed and said, "I took the liberty of RSVP-ing the governor's dinner invitation."

"Mom." I bristled. "I would've done it."

"When? A week before the dinner?"

No, the afternoon of.

"Hopefully by March you'll know where you're going next year. I'm sure the governor will ask."

Him, too? There was no escape.

Mom paused in the doorway. "I thought I should warn you, Faith's coming tonight and spending the rest of the week. Her mother has to go out of town on business." Mom lingered, surveying my room. "Neal and I were thinking about converting the basement into a home office this summer. Setting up a desk and a computer. We'll need to enclose Faith's area, maybe move her in here. Or lock her in." She smiled. "What do you think?"

I blinked at her. "I think on my way out you shouldn't forget to slam the door on my ass."

"Oh, Holland." She clucked at me. "You take everything so personally."

▼▲▼

I didn't want to go to Cece's PA program alone and I wasn't about to ask Seth. I called Leah.

"Hey, Holland." She sounded cheery. "I'm glad you called. I missed you at lunch."

"Yeah, Seth and I are working on this leadership conference." Which I didn't want to think about. "How are you?"

"Good," she said. "We never get to talk anymore. Remember when we had sleepovers every weekend? We never do that anymore."

"I know," I said. "We should."

"Kirsten's coming over later to have me trim her hair. If you came over too, you guys could spend the night, since we don't have school tomorrow."

"I can't," I told her. "I'm . . . busy." Crap. I couldn't invite both of them. I wasn't sure I would've invited Kirsten, anyway. She wasn't my favorite person these days. "I just called to say hi. See how you were. Uh-oh. My battery light's flashing. I'm fading out here. I'll call you tomorrow." I hung up. Damn. Now I'd have to go alone.

I flopped on the bed, scanning my closet. What does one wear to an evening of performance art? I heard Faith drag in, her suitcase scudding across the floor. She exhaled disgust. "Hey, Faith." I bounced to my feet. "You want to go to this performance art thing with me tonight?" I rounded the partition to her space.

She looked as if she'd been strangled by a boa, her eyes bulged out so far. "Are you joking?" Her voice dulled. "Or is your mom putting you up to this?"

"No. She doesn't know about it. I have two tickets, so I thought you and I . . ."

"Where's Seth?" she asked.

"Busy," I lied. "Everybody's busy." Did that sound like she was my last resort? Yes. "Okay, I don't want to go alone," I confessed. "I mean, I could but . . ." I smiled sheepishly. "I'm a coward. I hate to do stuff alone. If you don't want to go, that's fine." I headed back, praying, Please, please say you will.

"All right," she said.

I retraced my steps. "Have you ever been to one of these things?"

"PA?" She gnawed on her little pinkie. "Yeah, lots of times." Spit out a cuticle.

"So, what do I wear?"

Her expression didn't change. "Goth stuff," she said. "I'll loan you a crucifix."

I stared at her. Then burst into laughter. She was either the funniest person on Earth or I was losing it.

▼▲▼

It took me over an hour to find the Rogue Theater. The building was wedged between two nondescript tenement houses in the downtown warehouse district. "Lock your door," I ordered Faith. Check your mace.

A few people milled around outside, smoking and drinking wine from disposable glasses. They were not what you'd call the

116

"theater crowd," whatever that was. No furs or formal wear. More like grunge. Faith must've felt right at home. My stomach was jumpy, as if everyone else knew the rules of the game except me. The usher smiled a warm welcome and asked us to sign the guest book, which calmed me a little.

There was a small concession stand right inside the door with popcorn and candy and drinks. Faith made a beeline for it, but I snagged her trenchcoat and said, "Let's find seats first."

The theater was old, shabby, semirestored. The velvet seat cushions had seen another century. It was comfortable, though, and people were chatting and laughing softly. I read the program cover:

The Rogue Theater Presents:
A Night of Sensory Pleasure.

God, was this X-rated? The inside page listed six acts, and I scanned through them, trying to glean even a hint of the pleasures we had in store for us. "Singing with Cats" was the first act. Then "Virtual Virgins," "Synchro Nuts," "Aphrodisium," "Unity," and "Canned Laughter." I glanced over at Faith. She was watching me. I hated the way she stared at people, at me. "You know any of these groups?" I asked her.

"Hunh uh," she grunted, peering back at the concession stand.

I dug in my bag for my billfold. "Here." I handed her a ten. She scrambled out and I called down the aisle at her back, "No alcohol." A guy with a shaved head behind me winked. I shrank in my seat.

There was a page of advertisements, pleas for financial support, thanks to all the people instrumental in staging the show. Faith returned with a bag of popcorn and a glass of red wine.

Shit. "Do you have a fake ID?" I asked her.

"Yeah, but they didn't ask. You want some?" She offered me the glass.

"No." I visualized myself confined with her in a jail cell. Shudder City. On the last page were the names of the performers. My eyes skimmed down the list, stopped. Joanie Fowler. Why did that name sound familiar? She was a member of Unity. There, under Joanie was Cece's name. "She's in Unity, too."

"Huh?" Faith said.

Did I verbalize that? "My friend. She's in this group, Unity."

"Who?" Faith hung over my arm.

"Cece. Cece Goddard." I pointed to the name.

"Oh, yeah. I know her."

"How?"

Faith took a sip of wine. Savored it, just to irk me. "She's in my independent living class."

"What period?"

Faith blinked at me. "Third. Why?"

The lights dimmed and I shifted my attention to the stage. Independent living? That was a bullshit class. A spotlight illuminated dead center and a woman dressed in a gauzy full-length garment floated out from the wings. There was scattered applause. She folded her hands in front of her and waited. Waited. Through hidden speakers a cat suddenly wailed. The sound assaulted my ears and I squinched them together. The screeching ebbed a bit, then the woman opened her mouth and yowled with the cat. In harmony.

Whoa, it was . . . interesting. I mean, I couldn't do that.

Faith murmured in my ear, "Do *not* try this at home."

I whapped her knee.

"Do not attempt this in a dark alley at night."

"Quit."

"Especially if you're horny."

I couldn't stifle my snort. Virtual Virgins was a light-and-shadow show, which was sensual, all right. I kept trying to figure out if the three women behind the screen were really naked. Synchro Nuts was this eerie musical group that used electronic sounds and digitized voices. Aphrodisium was totally X-rated. Faith kept murmuring, "Ooh eee," and panting. I kept elbowing her.

The stage lights extinguished and the theater went black. Unity was next. My heart raced. A small floor light illuminated and a face appeared, followed by another beside it, and another until five faces stared out into the audience. Each face was made up to look exactly the same. But I could pick out Cece. The middle one. Together, they began to move, or rather undulate because, I realized, they were all one form. One giant octopus-like creature inside stretchy black fabric.

This sort of New Age music swirled softly from the stereo speakers as Unity pulsed in a circle. Then the music changed, became more strident, discordant. Each form broke off by unzipping their connection to the fabric and stepping out. They wore different pastel-colored bodysuits with hoods. Cece was yellow.

The beat pounded faster and the individuals, who were so serene moments before, began to jerk and writhe in agony. Cece opened her mouth, but no sound came out. I felt a chill race up my spine. This was no act. She hurt.

It went on for excruciating minutes. I couldn't watch. I had to watch. She mesmerized me. On cue, they all touched hands in the middle, their pain subsiding. The music grew slower, gentler, and the individuals moved toward the center, toward each other. Closer and closer until they were squeezed together tightly into one form, one unit, one multicolored being.

The audience clapped and stomped and I let out the breath I'd been holding. Faith arched her eyebrows at me and said, "Cool."

"Really."

After the show everyone congregated in the lobby, waiting to congratulate the performers. I spotted Cece with her fellow Unity members, laughing and jabbering, her face more animated than I'd ever seen it.

I weaved through the crowd to get to her. Be with her. Cece obviously knew a lot of these people; they kept hugging her and calling to her. An unexpected bout of self-consciousness seized me.

Cece's eyes met mine and her face seemed to light up. She weaved through people, under arms and wine glasses. "You were fabulous," I told her when we met in the middle. I had the strongest urge to throw my arms around her, embrace her, but my muscles wouldn't move. I sensed she wanted to hug me, too. She didn't, and the spontaneity of the moment passed awkwardly between us.

She glanced over my shoulder, searching.

"He's not here," I said.

She smiled. Smiled broader. "Did you really like it?" she asked.

"Yeah. It was fantastic. Hypnotic. Mesmerizing."

She blinked at me. "Did you understand it?"

"I, I think so. About the birth and breaking away and being alone. How painful alone can be. And then coming back together, being one. Being Unity. And the joy in that." I hesitated. "Right? Is that it?"

Another slow smile crept across her lips and up into her eyes. "It's whatever you want it to be." Her focus shifted to something, someone beside me. "Hey, girlfriend." Cece flung her arms around Faith. "How are you?"

Why hadn't she hugged me?

"Good," Faith answered. "You were awesome."

"Thanks." Cece's smile lit up the room again. She embraced Faith for a second time. "Faith, this is Holland," she said. "Holland, Faith."

We both snorted.

Cece looked from Faith to me. "What?"

"She's my sister." Faith thumbed.

"Stepsister," I corrected.

"No way," Cece said.

"Way," Faith responded.

"Wild." Cece shook her head. "Small world."

"Too small," Faith stole my line.

Another girl from Unity touched Cece's shoulder. "Ceese, we're going out back for a smoke. You want to come?"

"No," Cece said. "I quit."

The girl's eyebrows shot up. "You did? When? You didn't tell me that." The girl met my eyes and smiled. "Hi." She extended her hand. "I'm Joanie."

As I reached to shake it, Cece slapped down Joanie's arm.

"Well, thanks for coming guys," Cece said quickly, pivoting to push Joanie back into the crowd, away from us. From me.

What was that about? I was hoping Cece would invite us — me — to join them — her. Or something. Anything. I didn't want to leave.

"I'm starving," Faith said. "Those Canned Laughter dudes with the pork and beans made me hungry. Could we stop at Wendy's?"

Watching Cece hug another girl, I turned away and said, "Yeah, sure, why not."

Chapter 14

The ringing of my cell phone woke me up. Cotton-mouthed, I grabbed it off the dresser and grunted, "'Lo."

"What time you coming over? I thought we said ten o'clock."

I struggled to sit up, squinting at my clock. "What time is it?"

"Almost eleven," Seth said.

"You're kidding." I threw off my comforter and kicked through the rumpled sheets to find the floor. I never slept this late. I'd been dreaming — Aphrodisium had deposited a subconscious suggestion, or two. "I'll be right over. Just need to get dressed." What day was this? Why was I going over to Seth's?

"Forget it," Seth said.

He didn't sound happy. "Really, I can be there in ten minutes. Nine."

"Where were you last night? I called and your mom told me you went out with Faith. Like I'm supposed to believe that."

Uh-oh. Guilt gnawed at my conscience. Then anger overcame the guilt. "Do I have to report to you every night? Are you going to be checking up on me now?"

"No." He paused. His voice dropped. "I just want to know where you were, Holland."

My heart sank. Did he deserve to know? Yes. What was the big deal, anyway? Nothing happened. "Faith and I went to a performance art show."

"Why?"

"Gee, I dunno. Because it's there?" Did I need his permission to have a life now? "If you want me to come over, I'll be over."

"I have to leave for work in half an hour," he said. He expelled a long, audible breath. "Performance art, huh? Why'd Faith ask you? Couldn't she get one of her ghoul friends to go? Ar, ar."

Oh, Seth. I closed my eyes. "I guess not."

"I'll call you later," he said. "Or you could call me."

"Yeah. I will." We disconnected and I folded the phone closed. I should've just asked him to go with me last night, since she barely acknowledged my existence.

That wasn't true. It wasn't my imagination that she was glad to see me. I sensed a current of electricity between us, even with Faith there. Then that Joanie person showed up and cut the wire.

The phone in my hand beckoned me. I flipped it open and punched in the numbers. The numbers I'd memorized. One ring, two rings — my stomach knotted. I hung up. Stalled. Punched redial. One ring, two — just as I was about to bail, a voice said, "Yeah, hello?" I hung up. It was a guy's voice. I fell back in bed, then shot up again and redialed.

"Hello," he answered again.

"Is Cece there?" My voice sounded like a scared little girl's. I hate that.

"Just a sec. Ceese!" he bellowed. There was a short pause, then, "Cece, answer your friggin' phone." It couldn't have been her father; maybe her brother? He came back on and said, "Nope. Not here. You want me to have her call you?"

"No," I said quickly. "I'll just catch her later."

" 'Kay oh," he said and hung up. My heart was breaking every bone in my rib cage. I wanted to see her so much it hurt.

▼▲

Swimming. Up, down, counting strokes. One, two, three, four. Breathe in, breathe out. Touch, tuck, under, back. Her.

Everything was her. The light, the dark, the day, the night. Her. Her.

She was my first thought in the morning, my last thought at night. She'd taken possession of my soul. She was inside of me, consuming me, compelling me to —

What?

Drown it out. Fight the force. You can do it, Holland. You're strong. Resist. You can beat the forces of nature. You have to.

Swim. Stroke. Count. Count.

Can't. Can't. Can't.

▼▲

She was propped against my locker, waiting, sipping her coffee. When she saw me coming, she scrabbled to her feet and smiled. I melted. Today she had on a T-shirt that read: I HAVE A QUEER CONSCIENCE. DO YOU?

"Hi," she said. "Thanks again for coming to my program."

125

Keep it light, Holland, my brain cautioned. "No problem. Tell me about Unity. How did you guys get together?" I reached around her and opened my locker.

"A couple of us met in the theater department at Wash Central. I came up with the idea and put a call card on the bulletin board at Rainbow Alley. Why?"

"I just wondered." Light, very light. I grabbed my morning books, trying not to feel her breathing, feel her blood pulsing through my veins. "So, why did you transfer from Wash Central?" I asked, shutting my locker.

She didn't answer.

Hugging my books to my chest, I headed down the hall. She walked beside me. Close, too close. At the main intersection, we stopped. I looked at her, my question hanging in the air. A clique of girls passed, which wouldn't have even registered if one of them hadn't scanned Cece up and down. Eyed her shirt and sneered. Cece turned her back on them. "It was an unhealthy environment," she finally replied.

I scoffed. "And this one's better?" I found that hard to believe.

She gazed down the hall toward our lockers, eyes faraway. "Maybe," she said. "I'm waiting to see."

▼▲▼

We had a sub in calc who couldn't even spell "math," so he gave us a study hour. I could've used it to finish reading *Grendel* and start my comparative analysis with *Beowulf*, which was due next week. Or read the chapter we were discussing today in econ, or study for the calc quiz tomorrow. Instead I pulled out my sketchbook. Her eyes were so beautiful, expressive. The color of moss —

deep, dark green, but brown, too, around the edges. Wispy blond lashes. Eyes were hard to draw. Not the shape so much or the color, but the depth. The person behind them.

She was such a tease, I thought, smiling. Did she mean to be? She didn't like games; she'd said that. Could she be flirting? With me? Who could tell? All of this, her, she was an uncertainty. A mystery. Yet, when we talked, when we were together, she seemed so familiar. Seemed to know who I was, where I was coming from. She knew me better than I knew myself, I think. She was easy to be with.

And I wanted to be with her, like all the time. Eliminate the obstacles, the people and things in our lives that were keeping us apart: Brandi, Seth, Kirsten, society, me.

Me? Make that my fear. What was I afraid of, exactly? What other people would think? I guess, a little. But that wasn't what was stopping me from acting on my feelings. It was the intensity of them. The desire for her. I knew if I gave into it, I'd have to surrender myself completely. I'd lose all control. Everything I knew, everything I was, the walls I'd built up to protect myself all these years would come crashing down. I might get lost in the rubble. Yet, she made me feel alive in a way I'd only ever imagined I could feel. Bells, whistles, music.

▼▲▼

Mackel handed back last week's assignments. On the top of my half-face drawing he'd written on a sticky note: "F-ing unbelievable. A+." I must've radiated warmth because Cece turned around and smiled. Brandi snagged her attention by showing Cece her drawing and giggling, and I wondered if I could

127

sharpen a watercolor pencil to a point sharp enough that it'd penetrate a skull.

Oh, this is healthy, Holland, I thought. Contemplate murder, why don't you? Maybe you could hire a hit man to take out all the people in your way.

Okay, I composed a mental contract with myself, if Cece approaches me after class, I'll let Brandi live.

She stalled around looking like she might, like she wanted to. Then Brandi was all over her again. Where do you call for hit men, anyway? Dial-A-Death?

I found a yellow rose stuck in my locker vent after school. My spirit deflated. Seth. He always gave me a rose after we argued. Had we argued? He knew yellow was my favorite color. Yellow. Funny. I'd managed to avoid Seth all day, but I couldn't indefinitely.

What was I going to do about him? Tell him, of course. It was a betrayal to allow our relationship to continue. I realized now I only ever loved him as a friend. That the physical aspect of our relationship evolved because that's what was expected. A girl meets a guy, they fall in love, have sex, get married, not necessarily in that order.

Expectations. They ruled my life.

Cut the ending. Revise the script. The man of her dreams is a girl.

I was sniffing the rose, wondering how to let Seth down easy, when I arrived at my Jeep. Cece was leaning against the hood, arms folded, foot tapping. "Holland." She launched off the bumper. "Could you give me a ride?"

A bolt of lightning shot through me. Would she always excite me this way?

"Sure." I smiled at her. Followed her eyes to the pavement, to the flat tire on the driver's side of her Neon. "Oh, no," I said. "I hate when that happens. You want me to help you put on the spare?"

"I'm out of spares," she said, her voice sounding cold. "I just need a ride, okay?"

"Sure, of course." I unlocked the passenger door and she climbed in. I ran around to my side. "You want me to drop you at a gas station or something?" I lay the yellow rose across the dash. "There's a tire place not too far from here."

"No, I'll just call my dad later. If you could take me to Hott 'N Tott, that'd be great."

I switched on the ignition. The engine coughed. "Oh, crap. I need gas. I'll have to stop at home to get some money. Will that make you late?"

"No. Your house is on the way." Cece buckled her seat belt. "I'll pay you back."

"You don't have to. I need gas anyway." How did she know where I lived?

She asked, "Am I going to make *you* late?"

"Yeah." No sense lying to her. "But that's fine." I backed out of my parking slot. "I'll just call in sick." What? Had those words issued forth from the mouth of Holland Jaeger? She'd never blow off work. It was expected she'd be there, and be there on time. She was a slave to expectations.

As we pulled out of the parking lot, Cece remarked, "I had no idea you and Faith were related. She's really cool."

I just looked at her.

Cece laughed. "You are so easy to read."

Which made all the blood rush to my face.

"She's your stepsister, huh? On your mother or father's side?"

"Father," I said. "Stepfather. My mom got pregnant with me in high school when she was fifteen. She didn't really want me." My breath caught. Why did I tell Cece that? I'd never told anyone, not even Leah.

Cece frowned. "She said that to you?"

"Not in so many words." My voice sounded weak, same way I felt. "Her parents kicked her out, so she didn't have a choice."

Cece's eyes widened. "Wow. What were they, like religious fanatics?"

"I don't know," I admitted. "She never told me why. She hasn't spoken to them since. I guess her mom's written to her over the years wanting to reconcile; be involved in my life. But Mom absolutely refuses to have anything to do with them."

"How do you feel about that?" Cece asked.

"Me?" I looked at her. Back at the road. All these years. "I wish she could forgive them. Or at least let me meet them. I mean, they're my grandparents, you know?"

Cece nodded, like she understood. I felt her eyes on me, studying me. What did she see? A writhing bundle of raw nerves? After a moment, she said, "There's always a choice. Your mom didn't give you up for adoption, so she must've wanted to keep you."

I'd never thought of that. Why hadn't I thought of that? I'd always figured she just wished she'd had an abortion. End of problem. End of me.

"Where's your dad?" Cece asked.

"Who knows? Mom told me he turned out to be a loser and thank God they never got married. He didn't want anything to do with me. My stepdad, Neal? He's a good guy. He's the first really nice man Mom's ever met. He makes her happy. That's what counts. Unfortunately, he comes with baggage."

Cece shot me a dark look.

"Sorry, but this whole Goth thing makes me want to hurl."

"Why?" She shifted to face me.

"It's seriously demented." I smirked at her.

"Not really." She snaked an arm across the seat back. Almost touched my shoulder. One more inch. "Most of the Goths I know are pretty cool. I think the whole movement just got a bad rep with Columbine. What I understand about it is, they're into nonviolence, peace, celebration of life. Celebration of death, too. They try to find all the beauty in everything. Even pain. For some it's like this quest for immortality. For nirvana."

I stared straight ahead, letting her words sink in. Chastising myself for not even discussing it with Faith; not finding out what Goth meant to her.

Cece dropped her arm. "I think she's just trying to get noticed. I feel sorry for Faith having to compete with you."

My head whipped around. "What do you mean? We're not competing."

"Oh, come on." She twisted toward me again, tucking one leg under the other, her knee a hairbreadth away from mine. Her hand rested on her thigh. "All of a sudden, she's thrown into this new family. She has to share her father." It took every ounce of willpower to concentrate on driving, on what she was saying, on not looking at her thigh. "She has this new sister who's gorgeous and brainy and athletic and popular. How's she supposed to feel?"

My face flared. She thinks I'm gorgeous? "We're not competing," I repeated.

"*You* may not be." Cece blinked away. "You never had to."

Instead of the driveway, I pulled up at the curb and ground to a stop. Just sat there, staring at Cece. I felt as if she'd just skinned me alive, like she saw me from the inside out.

I exited the Jeep and Cece followed.

Mom was in the living room watching her soaps and giving Hannah a bottle. "Hey, Ma," I greeted her. "This is Cece. Cece, the Mom."

"Hi." Cece stuck out her hand.

Since both her hands were full, all Mom could do was smile. "Hello."

"And this is Hannah, my baby sister." I tickled Hannie's belly and she gurgled. Mom, I noticed, was examining Cece, reading her T-shirt. She said, "Would you get me a towel, Holland? This one's all wet."

"Sure." I lugged my junk to the kitchen and dumped it on the back landing. When I returned, Cece was sitting on the sofa next to Mom. "No, I just transferred to Southglenn this term," she said. "How old is Hannah?" Cece tickled her foot.

Mom stood up. "Shouldn't you be at work?" she said to me, snatching the towel out of my hand.

"I got a day off," I fibbed. "Come on, Ceese. I'll give you a tour of the crypt."

Cece got up and trailed me downstairs. While I retrieved the key from under my lamp and unlocked my safe — which I'd purchased as a precautionary measure against Faith and now felt guilty as hell about — Cece wandered around my room, fingering my things. Finger away, I thought.

She picked up the Dixie Chicks CD and smiled at me. I smiled back. Pocketing a twenty, I said, "Okay, I'm ready."

"For what?" She arched an eyebrow.

I shook my head. "You're bad."

"You don't know how bad."

"Why don't you show me?"

"Why don't you show me?"

A nervous laugh tripped over my lips. "Are you coming on to me?"

Her face hardened and she said coolly, "I haven't touched you."

It was true; she hadn't touched me — physically, anyway. In fact, she'd gone out of her way *not* to touch me. The electricity between us was palpable. Visible, almost. And dangerous. "Come on, let's go," I breathed, stumbling out of there. I didn't even remember driving her to work, dropping her off, or getting home. She hadn't touched me, but God, I wanted her to.

Chapter 15

We were deep into a drawing exercise on three-dimensionality when Cece casually moseyed by and dropped a folded note on my sketchpad. It bounced and landed on the table between Winslow and me. He reached for it, but I got there first. Opened it in my lap. "My mom's catering the KBTO Battle of the Bands on Saturday night," it read. "She said she'd pay you fifteen dollars an hour if you helped. My way of making up to you for missing work. We get into the concert for free, too. It'll just be the two of us. Wanna?"

Her handwriting was small, cramped, tiny little letters. I scribbled my response underneath, then got up and delivered it. I hadn't made it back to my seat before she burst into laughter. "Only if you can keep your hands off me," I'd written.

▼▲▼

Saturday couldn't get here fast enough. I put Seth off by telling him I had my period. That always grossed him out. I knew I had to break it off, and I would, when the time was right. When I could manufacture the words. So far I'd assembled, "Guess what,

Seth. I met someone I'd rather be with. Oh, here's the good part. She's a girl."

God. I could never do that to him.

Cece said to come to her house around four so I could help load and set up.

"What kind of concert?" Mom asked as I was getting ready to leave. She'd invited herself in after changing the towels in my bathroom.

"A rock concert, I think. It's a battle of the bands."

"You're going with Seth?"

I ran a brush through my hair, wishing it was longer so I could do something interesting with it. Curl it, braid it, something. "No. Cece."

"Where did you pick up this Cece?"

My head raised to meet Mom's eyes. Her tone of voice annoyed me. "You make her sound like a disease."

Mom lifted a college catalog off my dresser and flipped through it. "What do you see in this girl?"

If she only knew. "She's cool. I like her."

Mom set the catalog down and said, "I don't really want you hanging out with people like her. After tonight, tell her to look elsewhere for friends."

My jaw unhinged.

Mom added, "And be home by eleven."

Since when did I have a curfew? And since when did my mother choose my friends? I waited until I heard her footsteps on the stairs, then murmured, "Go to hell," and flipped her the bird.

▼▲▼

Cece's house was a couple of blocks from Washington Central, a remodeled Victorian, two stories, with a glassed-in front porch. Homey. I rang the bell, and a kid, six or seven, charged out the door.

"Hi." I smiled a greeting. He had Cece's cute nose. "Is Cece here? I'm helping with the catering."

"Mo-om!" he bellowed over his shoulder through the open front door. Then disappeared inside.

I caught the storm door before it swung shut, and let myself in. The aroma hit me first — Mexican food. My stomach growled. I'd been too jittery all day to eat. Too nervous, psyched. Cece rushed out from a rear hallway, lugging an armload of linens — tablecloths and napkins. "Holland." She stopped dead. "Hi." Her eyes narrowed at her brother, already zoned in front of the TV. "Eric, you turd." She shook her head at me. "He has no manners. Come on in. My mom's in the kitchen."

I trailed her through a set of arched doorways. The spicy smell was stronger in the kitchen and my mouth watered. "Mom, this is Holland."

Cece's mom straightened in front of the oven, daubing sweat off her forehead with an oven mitt. "Hi, Holland." She smiled at me. "Thanks for helping."

"Thanks for paying me so much," I said. "That's really generous."

Cece's mom slit eyes at her. "How generous am I?"

Oh, God. Cece —

Cece said quickly, "You can give her my share. We'll finish loading stuff in the van. Grab that box, Holland." She indicated with her elbow.

As I passed Cece's mom, she looked at me, examined me.

Made me feel like an amoeba under a microscope. What else had Cece told her?

A van was parked in the circular driveway out back. On the side it read, "Kate's Katering." Cece balanced her load on her knee and rolled open the panel door. We hauled in five or six long tables, then linens, dishes, silverware, cups, trays. Finally Kate — I assumed Cece's mom was Kate — handed us the last metal vat of enchiladas and consulted a checklist. "Go wake up your brother," she told Cece. "Make sure he knows what time it is. Tell him we're leaving now."

Cece disappeared before I could move. Leaving me alone with her mother. "You don't have to pay me," I said, fanning the flaps of my jean jacket, since I was sweating like a pig now. "I don't mind helping."

"How much did she tell you?" Kate asked, not glancing up from her list.

I gulped. "Fifteen an hour."

Her head rose slowly. "That girl." One side of her lip cricked up, the way Cece's does. Then her expression darkened and she said, "Be careful with her."

What did she mean by that? "I will," I said automatically.

A man emerged from the garage, scraping a length of copper tubing with sandpaper. "You have everything loaded already?" he asked.

"Your timing is perfect — as usual." Kate exaggerated a grin at him. "The girls helped." She reached around me and yanked the panel door shut.

I extended a hand to the man and said, "Hi, I'm Holland Jaeger."

"Holland?" He shook my hand. "Like the country?"

"Yeah, windmills and tulips."

He chuckled. He had a warm smile that extended to his eyes. "You girls have fun."

"You know it," Kate said. They kissed, then he opened the car door for her. Cece slammed through the storm door, baseball cap on and a blanket folded over her arm with a sweatshirt on top. Kate peered out from the driver's side window. "Do you *have* to wear that shirt?"

"Yes, it's mandatory." Cece sneered. It was her OUT! AND PROUD! tee.

Kate rolled her eyes at her husband. "Well, get in," she said with a sigh, reaching over to unlock the passenger door.

Cece said, "We'll ride in back."

Her mom's gaze fixed on the blanket, then she shot Cece the same look she'd gotten in the kitchen. "What?" Cece said. "We're not going to *do* anything." She didn't give her mother a chance for rebuttal before yanking open the side panel.

Cece stepped up and motioned me inside. There was scant space, with all the food and catering supplies, but Cece rearranged a couple of boxes and spread the blanket. As the van pulled out, we scrambled to sit. Ended up across from each other, legs extended.

"Isn't your brother coming?" I asked.

"My brother? Oh, you mean Greg? No, they're leaving later." She must've seen the confusion on my face. "He's going with his band. They're competing."

"Really? You didn't tell me that."

"Don't get excited. You haven't seen them play." She smiled a little. Then looked at me and kept looking.

My stomach was doing acrobat aerobics. "So, um," I shifted so that our legs weren't so close, so that I could speak. "I guess your parents know about you?"

"Oh, yeah," she answered.

"How do they handle it?"

She shrugged. "My dad's pretty cool. My mom . . ." She averted her eyes. Smoothed the blanket beside her. "She doesn't like it, but what can she do? My sister's a lesbian, too, so it's kind of a double whammy."

Whoa. "I guess so. Wow. When did you, um, come out?"

She fixed on me again. "To my family? About two years ago, I guess. My sister didn't come out until after I did. But they already knew. They had to; they just didn't want to believe it. Denial runs deep."

"Where is your sister?"

"New York. She's older than me, twenty-three." Cece blew out a puff of air. "It was easy for her. All she did was e-mail Mom back and say, 'Oh, Cece's out? Well, guess what? I'm queer, too.'" Cece flapped a limp wrist. Made me laugh.

"So do you bring your girlfriends home?"

She frowned. "Why do you want to know that?"

My face fried. "I just . . ." Why did I? Because I had to know. "Have you brought Brandi home to meet your parents?"

"Brandi?" Cece frowned a little. "No. Why?" She tilted her head at me. "Should I?"

My brain splintered. I felt dizzy, discombobulated. Out of my realm. Swallowing hard, I asked, "Aren't you . . . dating her?"

"Brandi? Hell, no. Is that what you thought?"

"Well, yeah."

"No. We're just friends. She'd *like* to be more . . ." Cece adjusted her cap, pulling it lower over her eyes.

"But you're not interested?" I ventured. Hoped.

Cece said, "She's not my type."

"What is your type?"

She peered out from under the bill of her cap. "Well, let's see . . ." Cece eyed me up and down.

I could barely breathe. Please, I prayed, do it. Touch me. Just once. That's all it would take.

She held my eyes for a moment and exhaled a shallow breath. "I like 'em hungry. Are you hungry, because I'm starving." She scrabbled to her feet. "I didn't eat all day."

I pushed to my feet feeling frustrated, let down. Cece dug out a couple of forks and we ate enchiladas directly from the pan. We filled the space between us with "mmms" and "yums."

The catered dinner was being hosted by the radio station for the DJs and their guests. We set up the buffet tables backstage in the auditorium and promptly started serving. The equipment crews needed the space, so we had to hurry. I followed Cece's lead, setting out and restocking metal trays, lighting sterno fires, cleaning up spilled food. What a bunch of slobs. It was the hardest physical labor I'd ever done, aside from swimming. At least in swimming you don't sweat.

By the time we'd restacked all the tables and reloaded the van, the battle of the bands had begun. Kate said, "Listen, I have a migraine. I'd like to stay and hear Greg, but I can't. You two want to stay, I presume."

Cece nodded and looked to me. I confirmed.

"If Greg can't give you a ride home, call your dad." Kate kissed

Cece. She touched my arm and said, "Thanks so much, Holland. I'll get a check to you as soon as they pay me. Oh, and Cece," she aimed a stiff finger at her, "you know the house rules."

Cece stuck out her tongue at her mom's back. As the van pulled away, I asked, "What are the house rules?"

She stared down the road. "Stupid. Come on, let's go hear the music."

We snuck into the wings where one band, DVOX, was just starting their set. The group was two guys and two girls, and it was immediately apparent who the musicians were. The guys sort of faked guitar playing, and not too convincingly. The girl drummer was amazing. As if reading each other's minds, Cece and I began to dance.

I'd forgotten how much I loved to dance. The only time I ever got to dance was at homecoming or prom. And even then only with my girlfriends because Seth didn't dance.

Cece jigged around me, rocking out, and my exhaustion evaporated. The walls dissolved and everything around us, between us, disappeared. It was just her and me. In our own place, our own time, our own little bubble. Nothing could penetrate it, no one could intrude. The set went on for like twenty minutes — one song — and by the time it ended we were both breathing hard. When a new group walked on stage, Cece groaned, "Oh, no. Are they next?"

It must've been her brother's band. "What are they called?" I asked her, watching them plug in amps and do a sound check.

"Pus," she replied.

I looked at her. "You're joking."

Her expression didn't change. They were introduced as —

Pus — and the first chord they struck, if you could call it a chord, made me cringe. Cece pointed out her brother, Greg, who was the lead vocal. "He's good," I had to yell for Cece to hear.

She said in my ear, "He sucks. They all suck. They *are* pus."

I laughed. She smiled. "Come on." She motioned me away from the curtain. "I need some air."

The fire escape door was propped open with a chair. We wandered out behind the building, where a couple of stage hands were smoking. They ground their butts into the gravel and sauntered back in.

Cece leaned up against the brick wall, one sole of her shoe against it to balance herself. Her head lolled back and she closed her eyes. I leaned beside her.

Then it happened. That electric current surged between us, through me, and tugged at my core. The pull was so fierce, I couldn't fight it. Didn't want to. She was close, so close, her head right next to mine. I could hear her breathing, feel her heart beating. The outside air was cold, but that's not what was making me tremble.

"Cece." My voice sounded raw, whispery.

"Hmm?"

I turned to face her, jamming my shoulder into the brick. "I want —" I stopped. Couldn't say it. Couldn't take the step.

She twisted her head and opened her eyes. "What Holland? What do you want?"

I was shaking so hard. Do it. Do it now. "I want to kiss you."

She dropped her foot, straightened up fast, and turned to me. "I wouldn't stop you." She wet her lips.

I closed my eyes. Opened them, reached out, and removed

her hat. Slid it down her back. With my other hand, I threaded my fingers through her hair. It was all happening in slow motion. My hand caressing her head, pulling her close to me . . .

I did it.

Oh, God. Her lips were soft. She was warm, hot. I wanted all of her. I was falling, falling, with nowhere to land. I had to step away.

She stood frozen, head tilted back, eyes closed. A rush of visible air escaped from her lips, as if she'd been holding her breath, same as me. Then she seemed to deflate.

She hated it. I did it wrong. "Cece?" My throat felt scratchy. I panicked; tried to restart my heart. "Say something."

Her eyes opened. She shook her head slowly and said, "God, Holland. What took you so long?"

Chapter 16

The phone rang three times. Just as the voice mail was about to pick up, he answered. "Hello?"

"Seth, hi. It's me. What are you doing?"

"Helping my dad put this entertainment center together. You'd think a couple of smart guys like us could fit screw A into hole A, wouldn't you? This is the third time we've had to take the damn thing apart and start over."

Good, he sounded normal, happy. "I need to see you," I told him. "Sometime today."

"How 'bout now?"

"Now?" My heart raced. Was I ready now?

"Any excuse to bail on this thing," he said. "You want me to come over?"

"No. I'll pick you up. Ten minutes." We disconnected. Upstairs, I snitched an English muffin off the breakfast table, shoved it in my mouth, and wriggled into my hooded sweatshirt. "Be back in a few," I garbled.

"What?" Mom frowned up from her reading. "Oh, Holland. Did you look at this catalog from Michigan? The campus at Ann Arbor is gorgeous. We should've applied there. They have a pre-law program. Of course, Stanford's law school is more elite, and that'd be perfect if —"

"Not now, Mom," I said, removing the muffin from my mouth. "I have to go to Seth's."

She sighed wearily. "Ask him about Stanford. And don't be gone all day. I miss you, and I want you to help me paint this stenciling on Hannah's wall."

Neal peered over the Sunday funnies and winked at me. I winked back. "Morning, Faith," I called into the living room, where she was sprawled on the sofa watching a *Buffy* rerun. She might've grumped a reply. "Hey, Hannie." I kissed her baby cheek, then snitched another muffin and headed out.

My Jeep seemed to slow automatically as it approached Seth's house. He was sitting on the stoop, petting his cat, Toby. Two-ton Toby. A stray that Seth had rescued from a Dumpster when he was a kid. So like Seth. When he saw me swerve into the driveway, he lugged Toby inside and sprinted across the yard.

I resolved to make this quick. "Where are we going?" Seth asked, leaning across the front seat to kiss me. I twisted to check out traffic, his lips grazing my cheek.

"For a drive," I answered. Where *were* we going? To the ridgeback where we went four-wheeling last summer? No, God, no. None of our old haunts. In my side view mirror Crandell Park behind his house materialized and I pulled into the parking cove. Seth rested his arm across my shoulders. "What's up?"

I opened my door. "Let's take a walk."

He unfolded his legs and clambered out. Sidling up beside me, he took my hand and squeezed. I squeezed back. At the barbecue pits, I stopped and lowered myself to a picnic bench. Seth sprawled out beside me. A couple of kids were playing on the swings, their mother or grandmother reading a paperback nearby.

There was no easy way to do this. I reached into my sweatshirt pocket, felt around for the cold metal and fisted it. Reached over, opened Seth's hand, and folded the class ring into his palm. "I think we should see other people," I told him. So lame.

He spread his fingers apart and stared at the ring. Just stared. Shell-shocked. Then his jaw muscles clenched and, blinking at me, he said, "What brought this on?"

"I . . ." I gulped. "I have feelings for someone else. It wouldn't be fair to you —"

"Who?" he barked.

It made me jump. "You wouldn't know h — nobody you know." My mouth was dry as dirt. "Seth," I twisted to face him, "this doesn't have anything to do with you. I love you. You know that. I want us to stay friends. You're one of the best friends I've ever had." Which was true. It'd never been the sex that kept us together. At least, not for me.

"Friends," he said. His head began to bob. "Friends." He stood abruptly. His arm flew out to his side and the ring sailed across the playground. "Fuck you, Holland."

I reeled, not from the words themselves, but the force. The venom in his voice. Frantically, the grandmother collected her things and hustled her troops together.

"Seth, please . . ."

He clamped his hands over my shoulders, hard. Bending me backward into the table, he said directly in my face, "Fuck. You."

My heart stopped beating.

He straightened and his eyes welled with tears.

"Seth. No."

He stormed off, spewing gravel in his wake. His fist scraped away a tear on his cheek.

"Oh, God." My head fell into my hands. It wasn't supposed to be like this.

▼▲▼

Cece was still in bed when I arrived. Her father bellowed up the stairs, "Cece!" then turned to me and said, "It takes divine intervention to get her up before noon." When there was no apparent acknowledgment that she'd heard, he cupped his hands and hollered, "Cecelia!"

A door opened. "What?"

"You have a visitor."

She peered down the stairwell. Our eyes met and her face lit up. "Hang on," she said.

She didn't have to worry, I wasn't going anywhere.

A few seconds later, dressed in baggy jeans and a baseball jersey, she charged down the stairs. Grabbing me in a fierce embrace, she breathed, "Oh, my God. I thought it was a dream. It's real, isn't it? Tell me it's real."

"It's real," I said, smiling. Feeling relieved.

She stepped away; studied my face. "What's wrong? What happened?"

The lump was still lodged in my throat, but I managed to croak, "I broke up with Seth."

Her eyes closed. She opened them and peered into mine. Questioning. "Are you sorry?"

"No. It just didn't go well." My vision blurred.

Glancing over her shoulder at her father and little brother, who were gawking at us from the living room sofa, Cece took my hand and led me out to the sun porch.

We sat together on the slatted swing, her arm around me. "Did you tell him about us?" she asked.

I dug in my pocket for a Kleenex, shaking my head. "I couldn't. I'm sorry."

Cece clapped a hand to her chest. "Thank God."

I blew my nose and frowned at her.

"I mean . . . well, never mind. I'm just glad you're here." She drew me close and kissed me. Made the heat spread through my body. A welcome affirmation that I'd done the right thing.

Conversation was forgotten for a while. It felt so right being here with Cece. I'd fought it so long and craved it so hard. I wanted to know everything about her, explore her, get inside her head. Strange. It felt as if I'd known her forever, yet at the same time, knew her not at all. And the adventure of finding her out excited me, like nothing and no one ever had done before.

Cece pulled away from me and stuck out her tongue. Not at me, at the window behind us. I twisted around to see Eric smooching the glass. It made me laugh. It made Cece scoot down the swing away from me. "What?" I said.

She gazed over my shoulder, eyes narrowed. "Mom doesn't

want Eric to witness my perversion. He might get the idea that two girls kissing is natural or something." She stretched out lengthwise, her head on the armrest, legs steepled over my thighs. I wrapped my arms around her knees and rested my cheek on them, watching her. Soaking her up.

Still glaring at the window, she added, "At least we don't have a double standard, which really pisses Greg off."

"What do you mean?"

She shrugged one shoulder. "I told Mom and Dad if I can't be myself around here with my girlfriends, then Greg shouldn't be allowed to either. Dad said I was right." She grinned.

I smiled. "You are so amazing." I wondered how many girlfriends she was talking about. "When did you know, Cece?" I asked.

"About you?"

It wasn't my question, but the answer intrigued me. I nodded.

"The first time I saw you at your locker," she answered. "January second. Six fifty-three A.M."

"No way." I wrinkled my nose.

She laughed. "Girl, you set off my gaydar like sirens."

"No way," I said again.

She smiled. "You did. And my gaydar never lies. Although later, I thought you might be bi."

No, I wasn't bi. I was sure of that now. The depth of desire — it was unbelievable. That, and the certainty of this being right. Being me. How could she know before I did, though? "How could you know before me?"

She laughed again. "I didn't. You knew."

She was right. I knew. I just never met the person who'd light my torch and lead the way. "Why did you wait so long?" I asked her. "Why didn't you just, you know, put the moves on me?"

Her face grew serious. "I wasn't really sure what was going on with you. I mean, you gave out mixed signals. Then it dawned on me, duh. You hadn't come out to yourself yet. I thought I'd let you decide how you wanted to handle it. You needed to be sure. You needed to make the first move. And girl," she flopped an arm across her eyes, "you were killing me."

I smiled. "What if I'd never made the first move?"

She peeked under her forearm. "I was prepared to get a sex change operation."

I smacked her shins and we both cracked up. The front door whooshed open and Kate popped her head out. "Hello, Holland," she said.

"Hi, Mrs. Goddard." I sat up straighter, giving Cece back her legs.

"Cece, you know the rules," she said.

"Mother," Cece clucked in disgust, "for God's sake, we're only talking. We're fully clothed. You can see our hands. Show her, Holland." Cece held hers out for inspection. I sort of wrapped mine around myself.

Cece's mom nailed her with a look before popping back inside.

"You're bad," I said.

"Well," Cece scowled, "she embarrasses me."

"Let me guess. Slumber parties are taboo at the Goddard house?"

150

A slow smile spread across Cece's face. "Ah," her head lolled back, "those were the days."

I tickled her into submission.

We talked and played until we were both loony. I hadn't felt this giddy since I was a kid at Christmas. Cece was a joy to be with. So fun. A blast. It was hard to leave her, but I had to. Mom might call over to Seth's, which could initiate a confrontation I wasn't ready to deal with yet. This was all too new, too intoxicating.

"I'll call you tonight," Cece said, the tips of her fingers curling over the Jeep's window as I rolled it down. I traced every ring on both her hands. We kissed good-bye and couldn't stop; didn't want to, until finally, *finally* I screamed, "Enough!"

It would never be enough. I cranked up the window. As our hands pressed together against the glass, I started the ignition. Started my life over again.

Chapter 17

I snuck up behind Cece in the lunch line and covered her eyes with my hands. "Long time no see," I murmured in the back of her hair. She jerked around. The others in line turned to look. Brandi's eyes widened. "I've been searching for you all morning," I told Cece. "I missed you at your locker."

"Um, excuse us." Cece smiled at her friends and sidestepped around me, being careful not to touch. Why? Over her shoulder, she added, "I need to get this algebra assignment from Holland. Entertain yourselves." She waggled a limp wrist at them. "I know it'll be hard."

Motioning me out of the cafeteria and into an alcove across the hall by the drinking fountain, she whispered urgently, "What are you *doing?*"

"Uh, pretending I love you?" I reached up to brush a wisp of hair out of her mouth.

She lurched away. Her eyes darted around.

My stomach fell. What was that look? Disgust? Horror?

God, was it over? Was this weekend just a mirage? A game?

She must've seen how white I was because she said, "Oh, Holland, no. Don't think that." She gave my hand a brief squeeze. "We just," her eyes swept the area again, "we need to cool it here. In school. You know what I mean?"

"No, I don't know what you mean. I thought you were out and proud."

"I am. But you're not."

"I want to be. I want to shout it from the hills: I love Cece Goddard!"

"Shit." She clapped a hand over my mouth. "We'll talk about this later, okay? For now, just cool it."

The hurt must've registered on my face. "Holland, I love you," she said softly, tracing the outline of my jaw. "I just don't want it to hurt you."

Hurt me? How could love hurt me?

She gave me a peck on the cheek and scurried off, leaving me hanging — longing, lost.

▼▲▼

She sat with Brandi in art class; didn't even try to slip me a note or catch my eye. Brandi glanced over her shoulder once, sort of studying me, but Cece said something in her ear and they both laughed.

It made me feel like I was the butt of the joke.

I didn't get it. Was this a whole new world with different social mores? Different rules? If so, I wished she would've clued me in.

They left together, Cece and Brandi. Like a homeless puppy, I shadowed them. If Brandi touches her arm one more time, I seethed, she's going down. At the stairwell, they split off, Brandi continuing up the arts wing and Cece taking the stairs. Halfway down, Cece twisted her head up to meet my eyes and smile. I didn't smile back.

"I hope you're planning to take more art classes in college."

I jumped. Mackel had ambled up beside me. "What?" I rewound the tape in my head. "I . . . hadn't thought about it." Hadn't thought about anything but her.

"You have a gift," he said. "It's rare and you shouldn't waste it."

The words tripped through my semi-consciousness. A rare gift. "Thank you," I said automatically.

"I wish I had your vision. Oh, how I wish I had your vision." He sighed and tramped down the stairs.

My vision? At the moment I was operating blind.

▼▲▼

Cece phoned on my way to work. "Can you get away later?" she asked.

The sound of her voice thrilled me. "Yeah, of course," I said.

"I'm working till eleven, but you could come to the donut shop, or we could meet afterwards? Go somewhere to talk?"

"Afterwards," I decided aloud. "I'll pick you up at Hott 'N Tott."

"Out back," she said. "In the alley."

"Okay." Was she embarrassed to be seen with me in public? Was that it? Apparently "proud" didn't necessarily follow "out."

I slammed in the house after work to find Neal in the kitchen, thumping Hannah on the back while she wailed. "Your mom went to pick up a prescription." He had to yell to be heard. "Hannah's teething."

I dropped my duffel and went to her. "Here, let me try." Neal transferred the baby to my outstretched arms. "There, Sissy." I rocked her gently. "It's okay." I stuck my finger in her mouth and massaged her gums. The crying softened to hiccups. Don't ask me how I knew to do that. Maternal instinct?

"Thank you, thank you, thank you." Neal pressed his hands together in praise.

I carted Hannah downstairs, where Faith was plugged into her death rock. She spotted me and doused a smoldering stick of incense.

So what? The whole world could go up in flames as long as Cece emerged from the smoke. I set Hannah on the bed, then changed and snarfed down the package of Ding Dongs that Mrs. Ruiz had slipped into my pocket at Children's Cottage. I dumped out my books on the bed to get a head start. Just as I was finishing the last problem on definite integrals Mom showed up. She tiptoed in, a finger pressed to her lips.

"Huh? Oh." I hadn't realized Hannah had fallen asleep in the crook of my arm. She fit so naturally there. "Seth dropped by earlier," Mom whispered, scooping up Hannah.

I lowered my calc book. "What'd he want?"

"To see you, I would assume."

Huh. I hadn't seen Seth all day. He was obviously avoiding me the way I was him.

"Faith, would you please not burn candles down here?" I heard Mom say. "It took me forever to scrape the wax off your dresser this morning."

Faith blew out the candle — audibly. As Mom was leaving, Faith said, "While you were in here, did you happen to see my snake? I can't find her."

"Your what?!"

Oh, Mom. I shook my head. She must've realized, or hoped, Faith was kidding because she sighed and stomped up the stairs. "Score," I called over the partition.

I visualized Faith's smirk. Then she said, "Have you seen my snake? She's just a baby, 'bout two feet long. Green."

She *was* joking, wasn't she? "Yeah, I saw her slither under your covers and leave you a little deposit," I said.

Faith snorted.

I crawled in under my own covers. All I wanted to do was close my eyes and recapture Saturday night. The kiss.

My phone startled me.

"Hi," Cece said. "Are you coming?"

Oh, my God. I'd fallen asleep. I blinked over at my clock. It was twenty after eleven. "I'll be right there. I'm sorry. It's going to take me half an hour."

"I'll wait," she said. "Just hurry."

▼▲▼

She was huddled in the shop doorway, the halogen security lamp casting harsh beams across her face. "I'm sorry," we both said together as she clambered into the Jeep and slammed the door. It made us laugh, nervous like.

"What are you sorry about?" she asked.

"Being late. I didn't forget. I fell asleep."

She scooted across the seat and kissed me. I kissed her back. Didn't want to let her go. "There's a twenty-four-seven coffee shop down the street," Cece said. "We can talk there."

I released her, reluctantly. "What are you sorry about?" I asked, shifting into reverse and backing out of the alley.

"Today," she answered. "I can't believe I treated you like that." She reached for my hand and held it in my lap. "Forgive me?"

"Of course." How could I not?

"This is going to be hard at school," she said. "Turn left here."

I followed her directions to the restaurant, the Blue Onion. When we arrived I turned off the ignition and sat in the parking lot, holding her hand over my leg, feeling her warmth radiate through me. She lifted my hand and kissed my knuckles. "Come on, let's talk." Her door squeaked open.

Only one table was occupied. Three women in scrubs, who looked as if they'd just gotten off work, were eating breakfast. Cece asked the waitress if we could have a booth in back and we slid in opposite each other. Cece propped her elbows on the table and spread out her hands. I intertwined my fingers with hers. I loved her hands. So strong. Soft. Loved all her rings.

"What would you ladies like?" the waitress asked.

"Black coffee," Cece answered, her eyes not leaving mine. "Better make it decaf."

"Make mine a hot chocolate." I smiled up at the waitress.

"You got it."

She left and Cece said, "I love you."

"Do you?" After today I wasn't so sure.

"No." She shook her head. "No, I only get up at the butt-crack of dawn so I can pretend we're having breakfast together at our lockers. I don't even have a seven o'clock class, you know. I dropped it after the first day."

"What!"

"Then I have to haul ass down three flights of stairs to pass you in the hall between third and fourth period. And I stall around outside the restroom by the art studio so I can watch you walking down the hall. I'm late to algebra every day. I love the way you move, by the way." She eyed me up and down. Then her eyes darkened and she added, "I tried to bribe that idiot Winslow to switch seats with me, but he's got the hots for you bad."

"You bribed Winslow?" I let out a short laugh. "How much?"

She huffed. "Twenty bucks. I told him if that wasn't enough, I'd have sex with him. But he still wouldn't move."

I burst into laughter. She disengaged our hands and started checking off on her fingers. "Let's see, I drive by Children's Cottage after school to see if you're there yet, to see if I can catch a glimpse of you in the window. I go by your house on the way to school. Sometimes from the library, I'd watch you guys leave for lunch. A couple of times I even followed you so I could maybe find out what you liked to eat. So I'd know if I ever, *ever* got to take you out . . ." She paused and glanced away. "But that was too hard, seeing you with him."

"Okay, stop." I had a lump in my throat the size of a watermelon. Thankfully the waitress brought our drinks, so I had a few moments to compose myself. My God, she felt the same way I did. Totally, unabashedly in love. We lifted our cups in unison, took a sip, and studied each other. Cece set her cup down first.

"We can't be together at school, Holland. Or anywhere people might know us. Know you."

I blew on my cocoa and frowned up at her. "Why?"

"Because I don't want you to have to go through the bullshit."

"But —"

She held up a hand. "You don't know what it's like. The locker thing was just a minor incident. Okay, it probably qualified as a full-fledged hate crime, but it didn't cost anything. Not like my slashed tires."

My jaw unhinged. "Somebody slashed your tires? Who? Is that what happened in the school parking lot?"

"School. The mall. You name it. That kind of stuff you can fix. It's the other things, the whispering behind your back, the laughing at you in your face, like you don't even have feelings. Want to know how many times I get called 'dyke' every day? Gee, I don't know," she cocked her head, "I've lost count. It's the ones who give you *the look*, though . . ." She shook her head. "There's so much hate in people. It scares me, okay? I'm really afraid of physical violence. That day at the juice machine? God, that totally freaked me. Not that I'm going to let the fear control me, or make me afraid to be who I am. I'm proud of being gay. But it took a long time for me to get there. I had to put up with a lot of shit. And I can't stand the thought of you going through it, through any of it." Her voice caught.

I reached over and fondled a ring on her index finger. Silver, etched with a zigzag pattern. "I can handle it, Cece."

"Well, *I* can't," she snapped. "Look." She flipped her hands over and took mine into them. "You only have a couple more months till you graduate, right? Then you'll be away from everyone you know. Not that society's any better, but it's easier to blow off complete strangers. Plus," she ran her thumbs down mine, "I don't think you understand all the consequences of your decision."

"It wasn't a decision. I'm this way."

"Whatever. You haven't come to terms with what it means to be a lesbian."

A lesbian? Is that what I was? I hadn't thought about a new self-identity. A label. All I knew was, I loved her.

She probed my face, my eyes. "There's a lot you have to work through, Holland. Trust me. This is going to hit you."

Hit me. I imagined being on the receiving end of all the sickos, felt the truth of her knowledge and experience seep in. Cece and I both took deep breaths and let them out. She withdrew her hands and, with her index finger, circled the rim of her cup. "I hate to even say this, but think of what your coming out now, in public, would do to Seth."

Seth. How insensitive could I be? People would be cruel. His family, friends, Coop. "You're right." I nodded. "You're right." I sat back, folding my arms across my chest. He didn't deserve that. My love for her had nothing to do with him.

"Promise you won't tell anyone?" Cece said. "Not yet, anyway?"

I met her eyes — her worried, panicked eyes. And understood completely her wanting to protect me. I never, ever wanted to see her hurt again. "I promise."

"Good." She exhaled relief. Lifting her cup, she poised to drink and smiled at me. "Until then," she said, "until it's time, I'm keeping you a secret."

Chapter 18

We tried to figure out between our killer schedules when we could be together. Cece helped her mom cater parties on the weekends and occasionally got a performance art gig. South-glenn wasn't going to the state swim meet — big surprise — so that obligation would drop off my schedule soon. During the week the only time Cece was free was after work, at eleven P.M. I suggested we meet before school, too.

"The pool opens at six and it's deserted down there until six forty-five or seven," I told her. "There's this faculty shape-up in the gym three times a week, but they don't usually get started until after seven."

Cece groaned.

"Hey." I yanked down the bill of her baseball cap. "We all have to make sacrifices."

It was hard staying away from her at school. She must've still been seeking me out between classes because we passed in the hall three or four times a day. Whenever we did she'd make eye contact and, without changing her expression, press a closed fist to her heart. It sent a jolt of electricity through me every time.

For the next two weeks I snuck out every night to meet her — our clandestine rendezvous at the Blue Onion. Afterwards, Cece called me on my cell phone to wish me goodnight and we'd fall asleep with the phone to our ears. It was exciting, like having a secret lover. She was exciting. My life amped up in volume.

One evening I floated in after work and Mom was at the stove grilling hamburgers. "Oh, yum." I hugged her around the middle. "I am so hungry."

"Something came for you today," she said.

"What?" I rested my head on hers.

"It's in the living room."

I wandered out, giving Hannah a belly tickle in Neal's lap. "Oh, my God." My feet skidded to a stop. "Are these for me?"

Mom stood behind me, wiping her hands on a dish towel. "Your name's on the card."

I'd never seen so many roses. There must've been two dozen, in a gorgeous crystal vase. Yellow roses, my favorite. My stomach dropped. Not Seth. Oh, no. He wouldn't. On the rare occasion we crossed paths anymore, he barely acknowledged my existence.

From the vase atop the TV, I removed the floral shop card from its envelope and read it to myself:

For my sweetheart. Together forever. I love you. C.

"Let me see." Mom extended her hand.

I slapped the card to my chest. "It's personal."

Mom smiled. "Things seem to be heating up between you two. I've noticed how happy you seem lately. Should I be pricing wedding gowns?"

Neal went, "Uh-oh."

My face flared. A pang of sadness pierced my heart. There'd never be a wedding gown. There'd never be a wedding.

As I lifted the vase, Mom whined, "Oh, couldn't you leave them up here for all of us to enjoy?"

"Maybe later." I smiled at her, then Neal. "I sort of want to enjoy them myself first."

Mom squeezed my arm on the way past. "Holland, I do have one concern." She held onto me. "This staying out so late with him every night — you're still in school, you know."

Shit. She'd noticed. "I'm keeping up," I lied. For the first time ever, I'd flunked a test. And I had a ten-page history report due tomorrow that I hadn't even started. School seemed so trivial now. Everything did. "I'm not spending *all* my time with him. Sometimes I just go to Starbucks to get away from —" I didn't finish, since Neal was all ears.

Mom cast me a dour look. But she released me and I fled.

Faith leapt off her bed when she saw me pass with the flowers. She seemed to be here all the time now. Of course, my sense of time and space was distorted. I existed on another plane, in another dimension. "Wow," Faith said at my back. "She must love you a lot."

My heart stopped. I set the vase on my dresser and rotated slowly in place. "What did you say?"

Faith smirked. "I'm not stupid, you know. This partition isn't exactly soundproof."

Every muscle in my body tensed. She'd been listening in on our conversations. Faith grinned, evilly, and retreated to her half of the crypt. This feeling of foreboding dropped over me like a shroud.

▼▲▼

Friday after school I slammed my locker, and yelped. Seth was standing there, arms crossed. "Hi," I said, taking a step back. He exuded anger. I'd seen him earlier at the student council meeting, where he now sat as far away from me as possible. Kirsten had snagged me after the meeting to ask what was going on between us. I told her, "We broke up."

"What?" I thought her eyes would fall out of her head and roll down the hall. "Oh, my God, Holland. When?"

"A couple of weeks ago."

Kirsten frowned. "Did you tell Leah?"

"No." Leah had called me, when? Last weekend? But I hadn't gotten back to her. I was a little distracted.

"What the hell happened?" Kirsten said. "Did he —"

"Yeah," I didn't let her finish. "You know, I really don't want to talk about it." I'd bolted, leaving her jaw dangling. Let her think he'd done it to me. Save his dignity, at least.

"I want my stuff out of your Jeep," Seth growled, jolting me back to the moment.

"Okay. I'm sorry, I forgot it was there."

He pivoted and headed for the exit. Cece had just arrived at her locker and either heard or felt the earth rumblings. We shared a grimace.

I scurried after Seth. When he got to the Jeep, he stood stiffly, glaring off across the emptying parking lot. I unlocked the driver's side and grabbed his sleeping bag and Coleman stove, a hockey stick and puck. I handed them around to him. Without a word, he left. He'd only taken a couple of steps before turning back and asking, "What did we have, Holland? Tell me that. Were you just faking it?"

Oh, God. I didn't want to have this confrontation. Not now, not ever. What could I tell him? Our relationship was a lie, Seth. I was lying to myself. But it wasn't an act with you. Not entirely.

What he was asking . . . the faking it part. Did he know the truth? Suspect it? My heart hammered. I opened my mouth to say . . . say what? There was nothing I could say.

Before stalking off, he nailed me with a look that made my blood run cold.

I sensed her behind me. "I think he knows," I said.

"How could he?"

I shook my head. "I don't —" The answer presented itself. "Faith."

"I wouldn't worry about Faith," Cece said. "She wouldn't tell."

I just looked at Cece. She didn't know Faith the way I did.

▼▲▼

Cece and I spent Saturday together. The whole glorious day. We went to IHOP for a late breakfast, then drove to the mountains and parked. An open space trail led into Arapaho National Forest, so we followed it, holding hands and talking, sharing our most intimate thoughts and dreams, sharing ourselves. We hardly noticed the snow begin to fall.

When we got back to the Jeep, I cranked up the heater and we started to kiss. It ended the way it always did.

"Cece," I whispered hoarsely in her ear as we huddled under a blanket in the back, clinging to each other and freezing to death. "I hate this. We need to find a place."

"I know," she said, still breathing hard. "I've been working on it."

"Work faster," I told her.

On Monday, a pink construction paper heart with a HERSHEY'S KISS rubber-cemented in the middle was taped to my locker shelf. She'd been leaving KISSES for me to find ever since Valentine's Day. In my coat pocket, in my duffel.

Over, with an arrow, was printed on the front of the heart. I flipped it.

Tonight my love, she'd written. *Meet me after work. WE HAVE A PLACE.*

My stomach did a triple flip. No way I was going to make it through the day.

Leah and Kirsten intercepted me outside the media center right before lunch. I'd been holing up there, hoping to stay out of Seth's way. Stay out of everyone's way. "We're kidnapping you," Kirsten said, clenching one of my arms. Leah latched onto the other.

"Where are we going?" I looked from Kirsten to Leah as they tugged me along the hall.

"The Isle of Bulimia," Kirsten said. "Otherwise known as my house. We're ditching the rest of the day and making chocolate chip cookies. Then we're going to eat all the dough and stick our fingers down our throats."

"No, we're not." Leah clucked her tongue. "We're going to give ourselves facials and faux fingernails. Maybe highlight our hair. We'll do complete makeovers on each other."

My feet dug into the carpet at the end of hall and we ground to a halt. "I can't. I've got an econ test today."

They both groaned.

"I'm sorry," I said, taking back my arms.

"Then tonight," Kirsten said. "I know you'd never blow off work, Mz. Anal and Responsible, but we'll pick you up afterwards."

"No." I shook my head. "I have too much to do." There was a drawing I needed to finish tonight. It had to get done tonight.

"See?" Kirsten turned to Leah, her hands on her hips. "I told you she dumped us as friends."

"I did not," I protested. Why would they think that? Because I'd been totally incommunicado for weeks? Duh.

"Kirs told me about Seth," Leah said. "You didn't even call me." She sounded hurt. My heart dropped. I should've told her. Made up a story or something. I hated lying, though. That's probably why I was so bad at it. And my self-improvement plan did not include becoming good at it.

"Why did he break up with you?" she asked. "What happened, Holland?"

What could I tell her? I became a lesbian? I always was, I just never acknowledged it? All I could say was . . . nothing.

"She doesn't want to talk to us." Kirsten lowered her arms. "I told you. She doesn't need us as friends."

"That isn't true." I did need them. Just not now.

Leah took my hand. "I am so sorry, Holl. I know how it hurts."

Kirsten snapped her fingers. "I have an idea. Let's form a club. The I'm-Giving-Up-Guys-Forever Club."

I laughed. That was funnier than they knew.

"I like it," Leah said. "Sign me up."

"You in?" Kirsten hitched her chin at me, then dug in her purse for a pen and her steno pad.

"I'm in." I smiled at them. Wished I could tell them. I wanted to talk about this so bad. Talk about Cece. About us.

Leah said, "We need to get together, the three of us. Seriously, I'm having friendship withdrawal pains. Let's plan a sleepover for Saturday night."

"Works for me," Kirsten said.

The bell rang and doors began to open along the hallway. People spilled out from classrooms.

"Say, seven o'clock?" Leah backed us to the wall. "Would you pick me up on the way, Holland?"

"I can't," I told her. "I can't come. I think I might be busy."

They both stared at me.

What did I say? "I mean, I am. Busy."

There was a change in the air between us, a drop in temperature.

"Come on, Leah." Kirsten shoved the notebook back into her purse and grabbed Leah's sweater sleeve. "We were right the first time."

As Kirsten maneuvered her through the crowd, Leah glanced back over her shoulder and found my eyes. Call me, she mimed, an invisible phone to her ear.

I pretended I didn't see.

▼▲▼

Cece was waiting, as usual, in the back doorway at Hott 'N Tott. I drove up and idled, but she motioned me to come inside. Not our usual routine. I parked in the alley next to her Neon and locked the Jeep. Then remembered my duffel and retrieved it from the back.

She embraced me under the security light. Reaching back, she opened the door and pulled me inside. "We have until four-thirty," she said. "That's when the morning crew comes in to start frying. I don't know why I didn't think of this sooner."

She'd been busy. Near the proofing racks Cece had set up a small table with a collection of candles. A portable CD player was on and this dreamy, instrumental music drifted around the room. It smelled like cinnamon and nutmeg and vanilla. Like her. Near the table Cece had zipped together two sleeping bags and added a pillow.

I looked at her and smiled. She took my hand and led me down. "I have a present for you," she said, kneeling on the sleeping bags.

"Another one?" I knelt in front of her. "You already gave me the flowers. It's my turn."

"Here." She held out a rectangular object. My eyes had to adjust to the flickering candlelight. "What is it?" I turned it over. No label.

"It's a demo tape of Pus. Since you like them so much."

I laughed.

"I love to make you laugh." Her lip cricked. "Here's the real present." She reached behind her under the pillow and pulled out a tiny box. It was wrapped in red foil with a mini silver bow attached.

"Cece —"

"Open it," she demanded.

As I removed the paper, she added, "I know you don't wear jewelry, but I thought . . ." She stopped and bit her lip. I lifted the top of the box to find a thin, gold chain. A charm hung from it. "It's an ankle chain," Cece said, taking it from me. "This is the Venus symbol, two females linked together for all eternity."

I examined it up close. "It's gorgeous."

"You don't have to wear it."

"Of course I'm going to wear it. Here, put it on me."

She motioned for me to give her my ankle, so I sat back and extended my legs. She removed my shoes and socks. Around the left ankle, she clasped the chain. I'd never take it off. Never. I pushed up to my knees. "I have a present for you too."

Her eyes lit up. I fumbled for my bag, opened it, and withdrew the page. "I had to do it from memory, since I don't have a picture. It's not exactly right." I handed it to her.

Her mouth fell open. She blinked and said, "Is this me?"

"No, it's this strange girl who keeps showing up in my dreams." I widened my eyes at her.

Her expression didn't change as she examined the drawing. "Is this how you see me? I mean, I'm beautiful."

I reached forward and held her face gently between my hands. "Yes, you are."

She flung her arms around me, clutching the portrait behind my back. "Oh, Holland. I love you so much," she said.

"I love you too," I told her. "With all my heart."

Chapter 19

*T*o look at me in the mirror, you'd think I was the same Holland Jaeger I'd always been. But I wasn't the same. I'd discovered this part of myself at the center of my being that made me feel real and alive. More aware of where I stood in relationship to others. To Cece, of course, but also to the rest of the world. Aware of what the world thought of me, what they could do to me.

Cece was right — it suddenly hit me how vulnerable I was. Because it mattered what people thought.

At my carrel in the back of the media center, I watched through the window a car packed with people careen around the corner and speed off. Probably to McDonald's or Taco Bell. I closed my eyes and sighed. My self-imposed isolation was beginning to wear.

I missed my friends. Leah, Kirsten, even Seth. I longed for the chatter, the laughter. I missed going out to lunch, going skating, going anywhere in a group. Not that Cece didn't fulfill my needs. She did. I'd just always had more people in my life.

"Are you saving this?"

I whipped my head around. "Leah, hi." I brightened. "No. Sit." I scooted around and motioned to the chair beside me at the adjoining carrel.

She eased into it. "What's going on with you?" she asked.

Blood rushed to my face. "What do you mean?" I ducked my head, faking an attempt to find my place in *The Canterbury Tales*.

"I've called you four times this week and you've never called back. What did I do? Why are you mad at me?"

"I'm not."

She held my eyes. There was pain in hers.

"Leah, you didn't do anything. I'm not mad at you. I swear." I crossed my heart twice, the way we used to when we were kids.

Leah studied me for a prolonged moment. "We never see you anymore. *I* never see you. It's like you dropped off the face of the earth. You stopped eating lunch with us and you never come over to my house or call me."

"I just have so much to do," I told her. "Too much." To prove it, I dumped my backpack out on the study carrel. "I'm so overextended this semester, it's insane."

Leah probed my face. I couldn't even hold her eyes. In a lowered voice, she asked, "Do you want to talk about it, Holland? Because, you know, I'm your friend no matter what. You can tell me anything."

A spike of fear lodged in my spine. She wasn't referring to Seth. She knew. Did he tell her? Did Faith? Was it my imagination running wild? Why did it scare me so much that Leah might know?

More than anything I wanted to tell Leah. My heart was ready to explode with the love I felt for Cece. But I couldn't. Wouldn't. "There's nothing to tell." I faked a cheery grin and shrugged.

"Okay, fine." Leah stood to leave.

"Leah —"

She slung her purse over her shoulder.

"I'm sorry," I said at her back, removing my glasses and rubbing my eyes. "It's not you. It's me. I . . . just can't."

She turned around. "We're best friends, Holland. You can tell me anything, anything at all, and I'll still love you."

Tears welled in my eyes. It wasn't that. I twisted away to the window. It wasn't that I didn't trust her.

"Holl?"

I reined in my imminent meltdown. "I'll call you tonight. Okay?" I swiveled back and smiled. "I promise. As soon as I get home."

Her eyes warmed to me. "Okay. I'll be there. I'll be waiting."

As I watched her exit through the media center's double doors, I acknowledged the lie. I wouldn't call Leah. I couldn't. Because if we did start to talk, I didn't trust myself to keep the promise I'd made to Cece.

▼▲▼

The weather was unseasonably warm for the first week in March. Judy opened the playground at Children's Cottage, and when I arrived all the kids from Dinosaur Digs swarmed me. "Miss Holland, come watch me slide," Courtney said, tugging on my hand. "No," Kevin cried, yanking my other hand. "She's playing with me in the sand."

"Whoa, chill. I'll play with everyone." I crossed my eyes at Judy and she chuckled.

After making the rounds, I perched on the edge of the turtle sandbox, soaking up the sun, basking in the glow of life. A blood-curdling scream at the slide shattered my reverie. Why do little kids always have to scream? I wondered, smiling to myself. Because they loved the sound of their own voices. I loved the sounds of their voices. A sudden surge of grief seized me. I might never have kids.

This pain ripped through my core. Kids. What about kids?

There were ways, I supposed. Weren't there? Adoption. Could we adopt? I didn't even know. Artificial insemination. Implant sperm in your body from some guy you don't even know? Ick. It almost made me wish I'd gotten pregnant with Seth. He'd be a great father.

Maybe I could ask Seth to . . .

No. What was I thinking? I'd be using him. As soon as I got pregnant, I'd be back with Cece. I'd want us to raise our children together.

What if I never had children?

"Miss Holland, you're squishing me."

I jarred to life, releasing my grip on Courtney. I wasn't even aware I'd been holding her. Reluctantly, I let her go.

▼▲▼

She didn't manage it often, being nocturnal, but one morning Cece showed up at the pool. I was just finishing a lap of back-strokes when I sensed her presence. She sat at the edge, elbows on knees, clutching a coffee between both hands. "What I do for love," she said when I touched in.

I splashed her. She set down her cup and dunked me under. The chase continued to the locker room, where I caught her and pinned her against the wall. Collected my winnings.

I snagged a towel and snapped her with it before heading to the showers. As I lathered my hair, I felt a chill prickle my skin. I opened my eyes.

Cece stood there, naked.

My breath caught. "What are you doing?"

"Washing your hair." She took over.

We started giggling and soaping each other and not giggling as much, when I heard, "Holland, is that you?"

I clapped a hand over Cece's mouth. "Uh, yeah," I called out.

"It's Bonnie Lucas," she said, her voice echoing from the sink area.

"Oh, hi, Mrs. Lucas." I grimaced at Cece. She peeled my fused fingers off her face.

"Your mom told me that Vassar and Brown turned you down. I'm really sorry."

"No big deal," I said. It was actually a relief, since it got Mom off my back for a while.

"They're hard schools to get into. Anyway, it's their loss."

"Right. Thanks." Leave, I prayed. Please leave.

"You know, you could always try to transfer next year."

"That's a good idea." I closed my eyes. Cece was doing things to me with the bar of soap that was making it impossible to carry on a conversation.

Mrs. Lucas said, "Would you like me to pick you up for the governor's dinner on Saturday?"

Was that Saturday? I'd decided to skip it, feign terminal illness if Mom asked. "No," I said, my breathlessness betraying me. "I'll just meet you there." My knees began to buckle.

"So, what other colleges did you apply to?"

God. I grabbed Cece's wrist. "I don't remember." The water suddenly spurt icicle cold. I wrenched off the faucets, still heaving, and steadied myself against Cece. Whispered in her ear, "Stay here." I pulled down my towel and wrapped it around me. Stepped out.

As I passed behind her, Mrs. Lucas eyed me through the mirror. Blotting her lipstick, she said, "You'll let me know as soon as you decide where you're going, won't you?"

"Definitely." I forced a smile and padded to the lockers.

Mrs. Lucas trailed after me. Her purse sat open on the bench and she dropped her lipstick tube inside. "I stopped by your house yesterday," she said. "Hannah's getting so big."

"I know." I smiled again.

We didn't speak while Mrs. Lucas folded and packed her sweats into her carry-all. That was a mistake; I should've kept up the babble. Cece emerged from the showers, tucking in a towel sarong. She skidded to a stop on the tiles when she spotted Mrs. Lucas. Cece's panicked eyes darted back and forth, trying to figure out what to do. What could she do? She scurried over and plucked her bra and jeans and T-shirt off the top of our combined stack of clothes, muttering, "Excuse me." Her eyes avoided mine as she circled the bank of lockers to the other side.

Even without my glasses, I caught the full impact of Mrs. Lucas's reaction. She didn't say a word, just clasped her purse and left. Cece's tiny voice echoed over the lockers, "Oops."

All day long I worried about it. Was Mrs. Lucas up in her office calling Mom? What would she tell her? What would Mom say?

I should've told Mom. She shouldn't have to hear it from Bonnie Lucas; shouldn't have to hear it from anyone but me.

After school I bumped into Kirsten coming out of the restroom as I was going in. "Hey, Kirs," I said.

She scanned the immediate area. Her eyes stopped on me. "Oh. You talking to me?" She palmed her chest. "I thought I heard my name. But that wouldn't be *you* remembering it."

I huffed a little. "I'm sorry I haven't called."

"I guess you've been busy. Having a gay old time, I hear."

My heart stopped. Even if I could've found my voice, I'm not sure what I would've said. My eyes left her face and grazed the floor. No! It was an admission of guilt, and I wasn't guilty of anything. I raised my head to speak, but Kirsten beat me to it. "I don't believe you," she said. "I guess we know now why you were so hyped about that club."

I felt like crawling into a hole. Why? I hadn't done anything wrong. "Drop it, Kirsten," I managed to rasp. "It's none of your business."

She exaggerated a smile. "Well, I just might have to make it my business." She turned and strutted off.

What did that mean? Was that a threat? What could she do? She scared me.

I stalled around at Children's Cottage as long as possible,

neatening bookshelves and stacking chairs. What was waiting for me at home? I wondered. I imagined Mom's we-need-to-have-a-serious-talk voice greeting me.

What greeted me was an empty house. There was a note on the fridge:

We're over at Neal's folks'. They wanted to get all the grandkids together for a family portrait.

Grandkids. Which, of course, didn't include me. She'd drawn a heart, and next to it: *Mom*. Underneath:

P.S. I left you fried chicken in the oven.

That didn't sound ominous.

When she got home an hour later, she stopped in to ask how my day was. "Good," I told her. She kissed the top of my head and left.

Maybe Mrs. Lucas hadn't interpreted what she'd witnessed the way I'd feared. Maybe Kirsten was just venting. I worried about it for a couple of days, and when nothing happened, I figured I'd gotten a reprieve.

Then suddenly, at school, everyone knew. Nobody actually confronted me, or said anything. But when I walked down the halls, it felt as if people could see it on me — a brand, or a mark, or a flashing red "L" on my chest. Their eyes lingered a little too long, and I could sense them judging me. Casting me out. The worst part was, I couldn't even defend myself. I wanted to scream,

"Stop it! Stop looking at me. I'm still the same person. You know me, you voted for me. It's me, Holland. I haven't changed."

This had the smell of Kirsten. She'd made good on her threat. Damn her. Why would she do this to me?

If only I could come out and be out. I loved Cece. I wasn't ashamed of it. I wanted everyone at school to know. I wanted the world to know. I wanted one person in particular to know. Mom.

It killed me to have to keep the truth from Mom. Every time she asked about Seth, this sense of betrayal gnawed at my conscience. I wanted her to know the truth. She was my mother. I owed her that.

But the thought of telling Mom terrified me more than anything. Why? We'd always been able to talk. Compared to most people, we had a great relationship. I just didn't know how to broach the subject, particularly after she'd ordered me to dump Cece as a friend. Mom and I had never discussed homosexuality, per se. I mean, it just never came up.

My promise to Cece protected me, for now. When the time was right, I'd tell Mom. I'd tell the world. I loved Cece. Mom would understand. Like she said, she knew about love. After she got to know Cece, she'd love her, too.

▼▲▼

The sleepless nights were taking their toll. It seemed as if my life flowed in one long, continuous stream — and I didn't ever want to row ashore. A person can live only so long on adrenaline, though. I could barely keep track of the days. One Tuesday or Wednesday, as I slogged home after work, dying to crash but knowing I had hours of reading yet to do before meeting Cece, I found Mom in the kitchen frosting a chocolate layer cake.

Had I spaced a birthday? It wasn't mine, was it? No, I wasn't that trashed. Mom's or Hannah's. No. Faith's? Neal's? "What's the occasion?" I stuck a finger into the frosting bowl.

Mom threw the knife into the bowl and whirled on me. Shoving me backward, almost making me fall, she said, "Is it true? Are you seeing that girl?"

My gaze flickered over to Faith, who'd stopped dead in the threshold between the kitchen and dining room.

I could lie to Mom.

No, I couldn't. "Yes," I said.

Mom's eyes blazed. "Are you sleeping with her?"

Oh, God. Did we have to do this here? Now? "Well, actually," I smirked, "we don't get a lot of sleep."

A burning sensation exploded in my head before I realized Mom had slapped me. Tears sprang to my eyes — more from shock than pain. "Mom, you don't understand." I moved toward her. "I love Cece."

She hit me again, harder, and I stumbled out into the dining room, my hip ramming the credenza. Neal was feeding Hannah at the table, where Faith slithered back into her seat. Mom charged me, pounding on my back.

"Mom!" I tried to fend her off, but couldn't. She was crazed.

Neal jumped into action. He corralled Mom from behind and said, "That's enough. We don't need to get violent here."

Mom yelled at me, "I didn't raise you to be a lesbian!" She made it sound like the filthiest word in the English language. "It's sick. Perverted. *You're* perverted." Neal held her in a death grip.

"It's not like that." I reached for Mom, trying to calm her, explain. "It's beautiful. We love each other."

She broke free of Neal and charged me. Hit me again; just started slapping and punching my face and arms and anyplace her hands connected. Neal wedged between us, palming off her blows. Trying to. "You disgust me!" she screamed.

I heard Hannah start crying. My eyes met Faith's across the table, where she'd turned to petrified wood. Almost. Did she smile? Mom said to Neal, "I want her out of here."

Neal said to me, "You better go."

"Go? Go where?" I asked.

"Go to hell," Mom answered.

"Mom —"

"Go," she shrieked. "Get out, get out. Get. Out!"

"Okay. God. Can I at least pack some things?"

Her face was so purple I thought she'd explode. "Two minutes." To Neal she said, "I want her out of this house in two minutes."

He widened his eyes at me. Hannah howled and hiccuped. "Oh, Hannie." I paused to comfort her. Mom ripped me away and screeched, "Don't you *touch* my baby! Don't you ever touch her again."

My stomach churned as I charged down the stairs. God, oh God. What was I going to do?

Pack. Pack what? Two minutes? I unzipped my duffel and started shoveling things in. Everything on my dresser came off in one swipe. What else? Clothes. The drawers were crammed; I'd never be able to pack it all. My closet, too. Shoes. There was no room for shoes.

"You have one minute," Mom shrilled down the stairs.

The roses? No, they'd have to stay. They were dead anyway. Let her enjoy them now. Faith, too. She could eat my dead roses.

I grabbed as much as I could carry; heard items dropping on the floor as I charged up the stairs. I felt humiliated and helpless and shaken. Faith was just coming downstairs and we collided. I shoved her aside, seething, "I hope you're happy. You have it all to yourself now."

She opened her mouth to speak, but I elbowed past her. I couldn't believe she'd done this to me. Did she hate me that much?

Mom wrenched open the door. Then slammed it shut behind me.

I staggered to the Jeep. Drove. Just drove. I was trembling and cold and my hands kept slipping off the steering wheel. My chest hurt. My cheek burned. My hip throbbed where the corner of the credenza had gouged me. The phone in the bottom of my bag rang, I think. Everything was ringing. My ears, still, from her screaming. I couldn't breathe. Couldn't see. Everything went blurry. Everything went black.

Chapter 20

Yeah, hello?" he said, the words clipped.

I swallowed hard. "I'm sorry to wake you up. Can I talk to Cece?" My voice sounded hollow, detached.

"Who is this?" he demanded.

"It's Holland. I'm sorry, Mr. Goddard. I need to talk to Cece."

He exhaled obvious irritation. "Just a minute."

My forehead rested against the steering wheel.

"H'lo," Cece slurred. She cleared her throat. "Who is this?" The extension downstairs clicked off.

"It's me."

"Holl?" Cece's voice rose. "I've been calling you for hours. Where are you?"

My throat felt dry. Raw. I sat back and said, "I'm sitting in front of your house. I need you."

A curtain in the upstairs window fluttered. "I'll be right there," she said. "Don't go away."

I laughed bitterly.

A few seconds later Cece tripped out the front door, her baseball jersey clinging to her legs, one hightop on her foot and the other in her hand. She sprinted down the sidewalk and across the street. Her palm spread on my closed window and she peered in before charging around to the passenger side.

"Holland? Honey?" She shut the door and turned to me. I continued to stare ahead. Unseeing, numb. "What happened?" she asked.

I blinked over to her. "My mother kicked me out of the house."

"No." Cece lunged across the seat and threw her arms around me. "Holland, no." She held me, burrowed her head into my neck. "Oh, baby, no."

"Oh, baby, yes."

Cece drew back. "You told her? About us?"

"No." My voice sounded harsh, the way my insides felt. "I didn't have to."

Cece frowned. "Somebody outed you? Who?"

"One guess."

"I don't know."

"Your friend and mine."

Cece looked confused.

"Faith," I said.

Cece shook her head. "I don't believe that. Are you sure?"

I nodded. I was sure.

"You're shivering. It's freezing in here. Where's your coat?"

I might've laughed again. "Guess I forgot it in the two minutes I had to pack." Tears burned my eyes. "What am I going to do, Ceese?"

She held me again. "Stay here, of course, with me."

"I can't."

"Yes, you can. Come on." She scooted out her side and ran around to open my door. Dragged me across the street and into the house.

Cece's parents were both up now. Mr. Goddard stood by the staircase as Kate wandered in from the kitchen, tightening the belt on her robe. "Holland's mom kicked her out," Cece informed them.

"Oh, sweetie." Kate rushed over and hugged me. I didn't think there could be any tears left, but a flood of them burst through the dam.

"She can stay here, right?" Cece said. There was challenge in her voice.

When neither of her parents consented right away, I said, "That's okay. I'll just go to a motel."

"She can sleep on the hide-a-bed," Cece's dad said. I saw him eye Kate. "We'll talk about this in the morning. Let's everybody go back to bed and get some sleep."

My eyes strayed to the mantel, where a clock read two thirty-five. How long had I been driving? How long had I sat in front of Cece's house? What day was it?

There was a flurry of activity and somehow the couch in the living room transformed into a bed. "This is stupid, Dad," I heard Cece say through the fog in my brain. "Why can't she sleep in my room?"

"Cece," he warned.

She muttered a curse under her breath. The next thing I knew

I was slipping between the sheets. Had I undressed myself? Then Kate was smoothing my hair — or was that Cece? And my cell was ringing.

Someone had enclosed the phone in my hand. "Hello?" I answered quietly.

"Hi, love. It's me. Are you all right? That's a stupid question, of course you're not all right. Do you want to talk about it?"

"Not really." I rolled over, pulling my knees to my chest. Shivering again, but not from cold.

"I wish you were up here with me in bed. I wish I could hold you."

"Talk to me, Cece," I said. "Talk to me until I fall asleep."

"Did I ever tell you about the time my dad caught me kissing this little neighbor girl behind our garage?" She chuckled softly. "My first love. Age six."

I smiled, clung to the phone, to her voice, until all the sounds in my head muted and faded and vanished into the night.

▼▲▼

Breakfast at the Goddards' was a mob scene. Everyone converged on the kitchen at the same time, grabbing a bowl and their favorite box of cereal off the counter. Spoons clattered and clanged as a milk carton got passed around. Cece stationed me in the chair beside her. Across the table, Greg said, "Hey," and hitched his chin, looking sympathetic. Cece must've filled him in. Eric pointed with his spoon, mouth jammed full of Froot Loops, and asked, "What's she doing here?"

Cece replied, "She lives here now."

"No, I don't." I glared at Cece. The tears threatened a rerun, so I got up fast. As I started folding the sheets on the hide-a-bed, I heard Mr. Goddard say, "Come on, guys. Get a move on." I felt him come up behind me and linger. "Hang in there, kid." He patted my shoulder. "It's not the end of the world."

Easy for him to say; he was living the American dream. The clock on the mantel chimed eight o'clock and I trudged back to the kitchen. "I forgot my money. Could somebody loan me five dollars for gas so I can get to school?" I couldn't help it; I burst into tears.

Cece threw her arms around me. From the counter where she was pouring coffee, Kate said, "Why don't you stay home today? You're in no shape to go to school. Cece, you take Holland up to your room so she can go back to bed."

"Really?" Cece's eyes widened.

"Alone," her mother intoned. "You both look exhausted, but *you're* going to school." She evil-eyed Cece.

"Mom —"

"No!"

Cece grabbed my hand and dragged me through the living room and up the stairs.

▼▲▼

It's a myth that things always look brighter in the morning. Every time I'd nod off and wake up, the nightmare was blacker. Bleaker. Too exhausted to sleep anymore, I just lay in Cece's bed, absorbing my surroundings. Her room. I'd never been up here before. She had a cache of stuffed animals in a net overhead. Stacks of

CDs by the bed. No closet doors, but the space was packed with clothes. Her dresser mirror had stickers all over it: pink triangles, rainbow hearts, and lightning bolts. A few photos were wedged under the frame and I straggled out of bed to look at them.

There was a family shot — Cece, her older sister, I assumed, Greg, and Eric standing by a Christmas tree. One of Cece in a short red dress, posing like a model. The other pics were friends, I guessed, a mix of girls and guys. A couple of familiar faces, though not from Southglenn. Where had I seen them? I removed one of the photos to examine it more closely.

It was a group shot. A rainbow banner behind the group read, "LGBT Queer and Questioning." The lesbigay club at Washington Central, had to be. There were six or seven guys in it, as many girls. Cece sat on the floor in the front row, hugging her knees. Her hair was longer, darker. Everyone was smiling or laughing, their arms around each others' shoulders. Cece was smiling, too, but it wasn't a happy smile. She seemed far away, removed from the others. It made me wonder again why she'd transferred.

But only for a moment. Thank God she had.

I put the photo back. Noticed a flyer on her dresser announcing a performance of Unity last Saturday night. Last Saturday? I frowned. Cece told me she was working on Saturday. Why would she lie? She'd never lie to me. The performance must've been canceled, or rescheduled.

The aroma of freshly baked bread swirled up my nose. Instinct and hunger took over. I wriggled into Cece's hightops and headed downstairs.

Kate was in the kitchen checking on two loaves of bread in the

oven. Two more were cooling on a rack. They smelled unbelievable.

"Hi, sweetie," she said when I hesitated in the doorway. "Why
don't you sit down and I'll fix you a bowl of soup. Nothing like
chicken soup for the soul."

My throat constricted. That was the book I bought Mom for
Christmas: *Chicken Soup for the Mother's Soul.*

Kate ladled out a huge bowl of noodle soup and served it up
with a plate of homemade buttered bread. She sliced me a wedge
of cheesecake, too, then sliding into a chair across from me, she
folded her hands on the table and said, "She'll come around. It
just takes time."

I blinked up at her. "You don't know my mom."

Kate cocked her head. "Do you want me to call her? I could
talk to her."

My eyes fell. "No." God, no. It wouldn't help to have my
mother screaming at Kate. "I'll deal with it. But thanks." I slurped
a spoonful of soup. It didn't taste like chicken; didn't taste at all.
Great. I'd lost all sensation. "This is delicious." I forced a smile.

Kate worried a loose thread on her sweater sleeve. "She just
overreacted. It can be a rude awakening, you know." The oven
timer buzzed and Kate scraped back her chair. "She has to get
used to the idea, that's all."

"How long did it take you?" I asked.

She either didn't hear or didn't care for the question. I watched
her remove the loaves from the oven and set them atop the burn-
ers. "It hasn't been easy with Cece," she finally said. "Not that
she's . . . gay." Kate faltered, as if it hurt to speak the truth. "Just

that she's so out there. I'm afraid for her all the time. I don't want her to get hurt."

She turned and looked at me, through me. I didn't know what she expected me to say. "Like the locker incident?" I settled on.

"What locker incident?" she snapped.

"Nothing." Shit. I stuffed my big mouth full of bread.

"Dammit." Kate folded her arms. "I don't understand why she has to flaunt her sexuality. It's a private thing. She should keep it that way. Be discreet, like her sister. I don't see *you* out there exposing yourself to the world."

Not because I wouldn't, I wanted to say. And it wasn't about sexuality. Not entirely. It was about identity. Love.

Kate added, "She's just asking for trouble."

I thought she was asking for acceptance. I almost said it. Good thing my mouth was full because now was not the time to debate the visibility issue. Not the time to debate anything.

Removing her apron, Kate let out a weary breath and said, "I want her to be happy. That's all Tom and I have ever wanted for our kids. I'm sure your mother feels the same way, Holland. We want so much for our kids to grow up and have all the things we never had. We have high hopes for you. Expectations, dreams. Then, something like this . . ." Her voice trailed away.

Something like this. Right. Shattered dreams. When it came to my mom, shattered dreams seemed to be my specialty.

Chapter 21

I stayed with Cece the next couple of days. My cell phone became my constant companion. I'd check it hourly — make sure it was on, the batteries charged. Mom knew my number. When I hadn't heard from her by Friday, I decided to stop by the house after work. If nothing else for more clothes, for the cash in my safe. I couldn't keep borrowing gas and lunch money from Cece.

Mom's car was parked in the driveway. My pulse quickened. Maybe when she saw me, remembered who I was . . .

The back door was locked, so I dug out my house key and inserted it into the keyhole.

It didn't fit.

I don't know how long I stood there, in denial. She was in the kitchen, behind the curtain. I could see her silhouette. She saw me, I know she did. The outline vanished. The message sank in. I stumbled back to the Jeep.

When I let myself in the back door of Cece's house, I heard

Cece in the kitchen with her mom, arguing. Cece yelled, "Why can't she stay here? What are you going to do, throw her out on the street?"

Kate said, "Calm down. That isn't going to happen, and you know it. But I called and talked to her mother."

My stomach hurt. I wobbled a little; had to brace myself against the pantry shelves.

Kate's voice lowered. "It looks like we're going to need to find her a more permanent place."

I felt like throwing up.

Cece said, "Mom, she *has* to stay here. Everything that's happened, it's all my fault."

"No, it isn't," Kate barked. "It takes two to tango."

"I don't mean that." Cece clucked her tongue. "I mean . . ." Her voice fell away. "It's just my fault."

"No, it isn't." I stepped through the doorway. "Your mom's right, Cece. I need to find a place to live."

"No." Cece rushed across the room and flung her arms around me. "I want you to stay here."

"Ceese, you know I can't. Not like this." I glanced briefly at Kate. "It's too hard."

Cece's face disintegrated. She knew I was right. It was agony not being able to be together. To hold each other, to kiss and touch and sleep together. She wheeled on her mom, but I pushed Cece out of the kitchen before she said something she'd regret. We didn't both need to be on the streets.

"Cece," her mom stopped us midway through the living room. "Come back here a minute."

Cece squeezed my hand and retreated. Her mother hugged and kissed her. It made my stomach heave and I raced for the bathroom.

▼▲▼

Faith was hanging at my locker the next morning. Literally. She was slumped over like a ragdoll, swinging her head, her stringy black hair sweeping the floor. This atonal chant was issuing from her mouth, sounding like a death knell.

Her own, I hoped.

"What do you want?" I said.

She jerked upright. Her head smacked against the locker with a clang.

Ow. Any other time I might've been concerned about a possible concussion. At the moment, I couldn't seem to garner much compassion.

"I just . . ." She gulped audibly, like she could detect my murderous vibes. "I wanted to talk to you."

"I don't have anything to say to you, Faith. Do you mind?" I indicated my blocked locker.

She stepped aside. I opened the locker and shoved in my duffel. I gathered books and spirals into my arms and when I shut the locker, she was still there. "What?" I snapped.

"Are you okay?" she asked.

"Oh, yeah. I'm great. Thanks for caring." I wheeled.

"I do," she said at my back. "I wanted to say I'm sorry."

Sorry? I seethed inside. Sorry doesn't cut it, Faith. Sorry doesn't begin to cut it.

▼▲

The next couple of evenings Cece and I checked the classifieds for apartments. The cheapest studio we found was five hundred dollars a month. "I don't bring home even half that," I told her. "What am I going to do?" Panic rose in my chest. "What if I end up living in my Jeep?"

"That wouldn't be so bad," Cece said. "It's cozy in there. Put in a TV, a lamp."

I couldn't even work up a mock sneer.

"Don't worry, baby." She rested her forehead on mine. "Everything'll work out."

Yeah, I thought. Like my life so far.

On Saturday morning Cece woke me by throwing herself on my lifeless form. "Get up. It's moving day."

I groaned. Our midnight phone chats were recalibrating my internal clock.

Cece said, "I don't know why I didn't think of this earlier." She lifted the sheet and wriggled in beside me. "You'll always have family now," she murmured. "You're one of us." She ran a finger down my cheek.

"Ceese, don't do that," I cautioned, covering her finger with my hand. "You know what it does to me."

"Get out of there!" Kate shrieked, propelling me into the air. Cece, too.

"We're just talking," Cece said.

"I don't care. Get out."

Cece flung off the sheets and scrambled over me. "Come on, Holland. We're going down to the Center to check out their

194

housing resources. Like I said, you have *real* family now." She nailed her mother with a look.

I'd settle for any semblance of real.

▼▲▼

The Center was the Gay, Lesbian, Bisexual, and Transgendered Resource Center. It was an innocuous brick building located in a strip mall next to a Kinko's copy shop. I wouldn't have noticed it at all if it hadn't been for the rainbow flag. On the door were two signs: SAFE SPACE and LOVE SPOKEN HERE. I clung to Cece as we entered.

A few people were gathered around a TV watching *The Price Is Right* and shouting, "Higher! Higher!" An older woman passed us on her way out and smiled a hello. Maybe I could live here, I thought. It feels welcoming.

I let Cece do the talking. She explained my situation to the receptionist, who kept shaking his head and saying how sorry he was. Sorry, sorry, sorry. I didn't need his sympathy; I needed a home.

"Wait right here," he said. He shot out of his chair. "Don't move a muscle." Like I could.

He raced around the corner and down a hall. A minute later he reappeared. "Go on in. Third door to your right." His phone rang and he answered out of breath, "GLBT Center. We're glad you called. My name's Terry. How can I help?"

A woman was waiting outside the office. "Hi, I'm Syd," she said, shaking our hands. "I'm the resource coordinator. Come on in, have a seat." She motioned us inside. "Terry told me what happened. I'm really sorry, Holland. You came to the right place."

Syd circled her desk and sat. "The Center has a housing program for street youths."

Street youths? God. I never thought I'd be a street youth.

Syd got on the phone. It took her a while to find a place with an opening. Everywhere was full. There were even waiting lists, which should've made me feel better, less alone. But it didn't. I just felt freaked. What if I ended up living on the street?

Cece reached over and took my hand. It calmed me a little.

"You do? Fantastic!" Syd held up an index finger. "Great. Thanks, William. I'm sending them right over." She hung up. "There's a vacancy at Taggert House. Here's the address." She scribbled on a pink message pad.

"Do you want to talk to someone about this, Holland?" she asked, handing the page to me. "We have counselors here."

"I'm fine," I mumbled.

"She's fine," Cece echoed. "She has me to talk to."

Syd smiled. It felt warm, wonderful, that she knew we were a couple. She gave us driving directions to Taggert House and we left.

When we pulled up at the building, I almost hurled. It was an old flea-bitten hotel downtown by the railroad tracks that had been converted to a shelter. A homeless shelter. Cece had to practically wrestle me out of the Jeep and drag me through the door.

"It ain't the Ritz, but hey. What we lacks in looks, we makes up for in love." The guy who managed the place, William, had a thick southern accent. Okay, he was sweet. He told us he and his partner shared an apartment on the main floor. "But the penthouse suites are on the second floor. This-a-way." He crooked a finger and bounded up the stairs.

As he unlocked my room at the top of the rickety steps, he added, "You're lucky. This suite just opened up yesterday."

I couldn't contain the gasp that escaped from my mouth. The apartment was a dump. Wallpaper was peeling everywhere and the furniture, if you could call it that, was all ripped and filthy. The mattress — oh, my God — the mattress was stained. The whole place reeked of mold and rot and cat pee.

Cece entered the room and wandered around, fingering things. William pulled me aside in the hall. "Okay, hon, here's your key. We really discourage you from making a copy for your girlfriend. We've had some problems with exes, if you know what I mean."

No, I didn't know what he meant. Like what? Burglary? Domestic violence?

He pressed the key into my hand. "Let me give you the grand tour." He crossed the threshold. "You have all your amenities. Salon, master bedroom, deluxe kitchen, den." His arm swept across the one big room. There was the bed, a rusty sink, an ancient refrigerator, a crusted-over microwave, and a fifties dinette set. I spied the door to the bathroom on my right and decided against a preview. "There isn't a lot of storage space," William said, "but if you need more there's a rental unit down the street. And if you want to use our kitchen for a party or something, just ask. We serve brunch on Sundays for everyone in the house, then afterwards we all gather for family hour. Just to see how everybody's doing."

"Is this the bathroom?" Cece asked. She popped her head in and pulled it out fast. The horror in her eyes spoke volumes.

William rattled off the rules: We were free to come and go, no parties on weekdays, be considerate noisewise. Not too restrictive.

I asked the question I'd been avoiding, dreading the answer to: "How much is the rent?"

"For you?" He sized me up. "Free."

"Free? Are you kidding?"

William winked and grinned.

For free, it was the Plaza.

"Until you get your feet on the ground," he added. "Then it's sliding scale."

"What's that?" Cece and I asked together.

"Means whatever you can afford. *You* just take care of *you*." He gave my arm a squeeze. "We have a philosophy here: Accept the help you need; give the help you can."

Cece said, "How many other lesbians live in this place?"

William replied, "None — at the moment. To be honest, we don't get too many women."

"That's good," Cece said.

What was good about it? I wondered. That I was a rarity? Oh, yeah, I felt so special.

"Wait," I said to William as he headed for the stairs. "Is everyone here homeless?"

He scrunched up his face. "Now, hon. You're not homeless. Are you? Ramon, is anyone here homeless?" he called down the hall.

A tall boy with dreads, who'd just exited his apartment, turned around. "Homeless?" he quipped. "Not us." A dimple dented his cheek.

"Get outta here." William shooed him down the stairs. "Everybody here is, what we like to call, in transition. Moving to a better place." He waggled a finger in my face. "You are *not* homeless. Now, when you feel up to it, come on down and fill out the paperwork. Oh, and I have some clean sheets and towels. A little welcome basket full of goodies from the Center, too."

"It's not so bad," Cece said as I shut the door. "We can paint and hang curtains. Buy some rugs and kitchen supplies at yard sales." The hand she dragged across the dinette table left tracks in the grime. She wiped her fingers on her pants. "Today we'll give it a good scrubbing down —"

"Not today," I cut in. "I need to be alone today."

She frowned a little. Coming over to me, she said, "I don't want to leave you alone."

"I'm fine."

She took my hands. "Holland . . . ?"

"Please, Cece. Just go."

She looked hurt, crushed, but must've sensed my need. She kissed me and said, "Don't worry, baby. Everything'll work out. Your mom'll probably call next week and beg you to come home."

I might've laughed.

"I'm sorry," she said. "It might take a little longer for her. But hey, look on the bright side." She removed her baseball cap and stuck it on my head, then pulled my face close to hers. "At least now we have a place."

After I carted up my meager possessions, shut and locked the door, I wandered over to the dingy window. My view was the alley Dumpster, where some old bag lady was picking through the garbage. Yesterday, I thought, I was Holland Jaeger, regular person, regular life. I had a home, a family, a history. Today I'm . . .

I don't know what I am, where I am, who I am.

I checked to make sure my phone was on, the batteries charged. I set it on the microwave. Without warning, a ground swell of sorrow overwhelmed me and my bones disintegrated. I slid down the wall to the floor, bawling into my hands.

Chapter 22

Cece and I scoured the apartment from top to bottom on Sunday. Either the Lysol fumes made me lightheaded, or being busy staved off my depression. "Mom's sending over more sheets and blankets and towels," Cece said. "Kitchen stuff, too. I think she feels guilty about abandoning you."

"Don't." I stopped scraping the gunk off the microwave to look at her. "Your mom's great. You're lucky and you know it."

Cece dipped her sponge into the bucket and continued scrubbing the wall.

"I was going to ask your mom . . ." I swallowed hard. "Never mind."

"Ask her what?"

I sighed. "If she'd hire me part-time. I'm going to need more money. I'll need to buy food and toothpaste and shampoo, everything. My job at Children's Cottage pays like crap."

"I wish you'd told me you were thinking about that." Cece swept a cobweb off her head. "Mom just hired a part-time helper. But," she snapped her fingers, "I bet my uncle would hire you at

Hott 'N Tott. He's always looking for people to work the early shift."

"Yeah?" My hopes soared. "That'd be great."

"I'll talk to him tonight."

I voiced my next thought: "I might have to quit school."

Cece spun around. "No. What are you talking about? You can't quit. You have to graduate. You *have* to. What kind of example would it set if the student body president dropped out?"

I rolled my eyes. "Who cares?"

She flung her sponge into the bucket and charged across the room. Clenching my arms, she spun me around to face her and said, "I care. You have to graduate. You have to go to college. You have to think about your future."

"You sound like my mother."

"Oh, puhllease —" Cece paused. She bit her lip. "You're not serious, are you? You wouldn't really quit school because of this. Because of . . . me?"

"It's not because of you. It's not your fault."

"Holland," she said, shaking me, "don't do it. Don't do anything you'll regret."

Like promising to keep us a secret? I didn't say it. Her tightening grip was hurting my arms and I twisted away. "I probably won't quit," I muttered.

"Promise."

When I didn't right away, Cece said in my face, "Promise!"

"Okay, I promise." Geez.

Smiling, she patted my arms and said, "That's my girl."

Why did she make me feel like she was my mother and father

and friend and lover all rolled into one? Because she was. She was my everything. "What are you doing next year?" I asked as she returned to her bucket. "Staying at Southglenn or going back to Wash Central?"

"I'm never going back there," she said. "I can't."

Can't? "What do you mean?"

She replied, "Turn up the radio. I love this song."

I amped the volume on the portable radio Cece had brought over. She began to dance and rock out, obviously avoiding the question.

I resumed scraping. That solved one problem, anyway. I wasn't leaving to go to college out of state — if I was going at all. Right now college was the furthest thing from my mind. Surviving day to day took priority.

The song finished and Cece's sponge plopped in the water. She flung herself backward across the bed and said in a yawn, "Let's go get a pizza or something. I'm wiped."

I set my knife on top of the microwave, trudged over, and sprawled out beside her. We gazed up into the cracked and blistered ceiling. Facing her, I said, "You want to try it out?"

A slow smile snaked across her lips. "I thought you'd never ask."

▼▲▼

Quitting school was never an option, really. Well, maybe it was, but there were only eight weeks left. No sense throwing it all away, like *Mom* had. Like *her* life was so ruined. *Her* future destroyed.

203

The resentment, the anger toward her began to consume me and I couldn't let it. I had three midterms and a presentation next week, not to mention the leadership conference. Seth had gone ahead and organized the whole event, which I felt guilty as hell about. I wanted to thank him, to tell him he'd done a fantastic job, but try to talk to him. He acted like I was the Scourge.

Art class was my salvation. I could totally zone while Mackel assumed I was visualizing the next Sistine Chapel. Occasionally, Cece would glance back at me, looking worried, and press a fist to her heart, making me squeal with ecstasy. On the inside only, of course.

One Friday afternoon, feeling wasted from all the stress and overwork, I slid into my seat in art and ran through my usual routine: Check the phone, pull out my sketchbook, stare at the back of Cece's head. Mackel showed us slides of various objects and talked about how to draw perspective. How to give dimension to buildings, rooms, furniture.

A vision came to me. My dump. I dug out a pencil and began to sketch it. That was depressing. I ripped out the page.

Mackel eyed me. I grimaced an apology. What about drawing my vision of what the room *could* be?

Okay, it had possibilities. See beyond the surface, Mackel had said.

The act of creating, of transferring my altered vision to the page was oddly comforting. Possibilities. They were there.

▼▲▼

We were sitting in a booth sharing a box of donut shards and refilling napkin holders when Cece looked up and smiled. I twisted around. Faith stood at the counter, hangdog. "I brought your stuff," she grumbled, shoving a couple of Hefty trash bags at me.

So this is what my life has been reduced to, I thought.

Faith added, "She was going to throw it all out."

An ache gnawed at my core. "Is my safe in there?" I sniped.

"No," Faith said. "She kept that. She said . . ." Faith stopped.

My eyes narrowed. "She said what?"

Faith stuck her thumbnail in her mouth and started chewing.

"Never mind. I can guess." Even though she'd never actually voiced the sentiment, I knew Mom felt that everything I had I owed to her. "How did you know where to find me?" I asked Faith.

She and Cece exchanged glances. I glared at Cece. "I think I hear the cinnamon rolls rising," she said, sliding out fast. "You two talk. You need each other." She touched Faith's shoulder and added, "Tell her."

My glare engulfed Faith. "Tell me what? Why you outed me?"

"I didn't." Faith spit out a cuticle. "I'd never do that."

I held her eyes.

She lowered her hand and repeated, "I didn't do it."

"But you apologized."

"What?" Her eyebrows twitched. "Oh, yeah. For not defending you that night, not taking your side. I should have. It all just happened so fast."

I studied her face, searching for the truth and getting nothing but a vacant sign. "Sit down." I motioned to the plasti-seat Cece had vacated.

Faith scootched in. I offered her a donut chunk from the box. She shook her head, then stuck her thumb in her mouth and began nibbling again.

"It's hard to talk to you when you're doing that," I told her.

She dropped her hand. "Don't be mad at Cece," she said. "I made her tell me how to find you. I've been worried about you."

She was worried about me? My shoulders slumped. At least somebody was. I felt guilty. For blaming her, for cursing her every time I crunched a cockroach in my bathroom. "So," I said, forcing a smile, "how are you? How's everything?"

She met my eyes. Stuck out her tongue in a gag.

"Do you know who told her about me?"

Faith's eyes grazed the table. "I think so."

I waited. She didn't volunteer the information. I wanted to lunge at her, grab her around the neck, force her to look at me, talk to me, tell me —

Tell me what? That none of this had happened? That it was all her fault? Somebody else's fault? Anyone's but mine? Because it was mine. It did happen. The actions, the decisions, the consequences, they were all my responsibility.

Accept it, Holland, my inner voice admonished. Get over it.

I was dealing. Still, I had to know. "Was it Bonnie Lucas?"

Faith curled a lip. "Who?"

"Mom's friend. The career counselor at school."

"I don't know her."

Another long, uncomfortable pause. Was I going to have to beat it out of Faith? Because I would —

"Your mom called around to all your friends one Saturday to find you. You were supposed to go shopping for a dress or something?"

Oh, shit, the dress, which I'd agreed to buy under the false pre-

206

tense I'd wear it to the governor's dinner. Which I never did attend. After I became a homeless street urchin, dinner with the gov seemed a tad trifling.

"Kirsten," I seethed aloud. "I should've known."

"No. Kirsten wasn't home," Faith said. "Leah was. She talked to Leah for a couple of minutes. Then she called someone else. I heard your mom say, 'What girlfriend?' I'm pretty sure she was talking to Seth."

"Seth?" My jaw unhinged. "But . . ." No, he wouldn't tell my mother. It'd reflect on him. He wouldn't tell anyone. Would he? Is he the one who told Leah and Kirsten? Is he the one who leaked it to the world?

"After she hung up, your mom was like flaming all over the house. Totally psycho. She attacked me on the sofa and screamed at me to tell her what I knew. But I didn't. I swear. So she went through your room, trying to find something. Proof, I guess. She's always pawing through your stuff, you know. Going through your drawers and your closet."

"You're kidding." I knew she went in to gather laundry.

"Nope." Faith helped herself to a donut chunk and added, "Anyway, I think she found what she was looking for. A card? Something like that." She nibbled on a chocolate sprinkle.

"The card from the flowers. But I put that in my safe."

"So? She gets in there, too. And she checks your pills every day."

"What!" I gawked at Faith. "My birth control pills?"

"Mmm-hmm."

"But that doesn't prove —"

207

A horn honked outside and Faith flinched. She shoved the rest of the donut into her mouth and garbled, "I gotta go. Dad's waiting."

My eyes followed hers out the window to the parking lot, where Neal sat in his Ford Explorer, tapping the steering wheel impatiently. When our eyes met, he smiled stupidly. "Faith." I caught her arm on the way by. "I'm sorry." I stood up and folded her in an embrace. "I'm really sorry."

"Me too," she said.

"I wish it could've been different between us. I wish I'd . . ." Tears stung my eyes. I wish I'd been more of a sister to you, I wanted to say. Even a friend. I wish I'd trusted you. But no, I took one look at you and slapped on a label. Freak. Weirdo. I never once made an effort to dig beneath the surface. I was such a hypocrite. No wonder she couldn't stand me.

"Yeah," she said, "I wish I woulda stolen that Dixie Chicks CD when I had the chance." Faith stuck out her tongue in a gag.

I smacked her arm.

She added with a smile, "I really like Cece. I'm glad for you."

She was the only person who'd ever said that, and I needed to hear it so badly. I hugged her again, fiercely. "Do something for me, will you?" I asked.

"Anything," Faith said. "I'd do anything for you."

My throat caught. "Just . . . give Hannah a kiss for me?"

"Oh, I have been. I talk about you all the time, especially in front of your mother." Faith smirked. "I won't let Hannah forget you."

In my blur of tears, Faith disappeared.

I missed the blowout. Cece said she and her parents had a knock-down-drag-out when she told them she wanted to stay with me at Taggert House. They absolutely refused. Cece threatened to run away. She told them they'd have to call the cops to haul her ass back home, then lock her in her room at night to keep her there.

So they compromised. What choice did they have? Cece could sleep over on the weekends, Friday and Saturday nights. Her parents had to hate me. They had to blame me for causing a rupture in their family.

I lay in my lumpy bed, listening to the creaking walls, to the flushing of a toilet downstairs. A train whistle mourned in the distance. Cece had come in late, looking exhilarated and babbling for an hour before finally crashing. Everything seemed normal with her, perfect. But I knew she was a good actress. I wanted to confront her about where she'd been tonight.

She had told me she was working, that her uncle had called and asked her to fill in for one of the cooks who was sick. I thought I'd surprise her. Stop in with a Starbucks espresso, her favorite. Pure sludge. It cost too much for coffee, but it'd be worth it to see her face light up.

Except, she wasn't working. The regular staff was all there. The trace of stage makeup around her hairline was telling.

I rolled over onto my back. Why was she lying to me? What was going on? After that first show, Cece never wanted me around when Unity was rehearsing or performing. She never once introduced me to her friends. Why? What was the chance it'd get back to Southglenn? Wasn't she proud of me? Was that it? I wasn't gay enough?

What if she'd rather be with "them" than me? What if she left me? The thought of it made my stomach hurt. Cece was all I had. Without her, I'd be totally alone in the world.

Oh, God. I probed her gentle face, her receptive dream state. What would I do without you?

Stop it, my brain screamed. She's here with you now. That's what matters.

I took a deep breath to quell my anxiety. Try to. I needed her. Cece was a part of me now. The me that felt solid and sure and strong. She was the one thing in my life that kept me going, made me happy.

And that happiness hadn't come without a price. I'd given up a lot to be with Cece: my home, friends, family. Maybe even my future family. Plus this sense of belonging I'd always had. The sense of fitting in, knowing where I stood. It might not be so bad if I could be like her. Out. Proud. With a new place of belonging in the gay community. With new friends. A new family.

But what I'd lost was insignificant compared to what I'd found. Me. The missing part of myself. And Cece. Knowing love. Being loved.

"Please, God," I whispered into the night. "Let me be loved."

Beside me, Cece whimpered a little and rolled onto her side. She snaked an arm around my hip and pulled me close. Cece gave me life, she nurtured me, and I burrowed into the warm cocoon of her.

▼▲▼

Mr. Olander started off the student council meeting with an announcement: Prom had to be moved back two weeks because the ballroom we usually rented at the Oxford Hotel wasn't through being refurbished.

Prom. I glanced down the table at Seth, who avoided eye contact not only with me but with everyone else. I'm sorry, I sent him a mental message. Please forgive me?

If his dead expression was any indication, his mind was closed to mental telepathy.

After the meeting I had to make a pit stop before art. Exiting the stall, I found Kirsten at the mirror, brushing her hair. "Hello, Holland," she said. Her tone of voice made me tense. "Would you mind if I went to the prom with Seth?"

"He *asked* you?" My voice rose an octave.

Her face hardened.

"I didn't mean that the way it sounded." Or did I?

"I'm going to ask him." She pulled her hair up into a ponytail. "I think he should experience what it's like doing it with someone other than a queer."

All the blood rushed to my face. "That isn't funny, Kirsten."

"Oh, was it meant to be?" she asked.

I started for the door.

"Players," she said at my back. "Let's talk about players."

I closed my eyes. "Leave it alone, Kirsten."

"At least I only play one side of the fence."

I whirled on her. "Shut up." My ragged breath betrayed me. "I broke up with Seth, okay? I'm free to do as I please."

She cocked her head. "So you are." Hoisting her purse onto her shoulder, she shoved by me out the door. Halfway through, she twisted back and added, "And now we all know what your pleasure is. Dyke."

Thank God I was still in the restroom because next thing I knew I was heaving in the toilet.

I didn't think my day could get any worse, then Winslow asked me to the prom. At first I just stared at him, stunned. When my voice returned, I stammered, "Wow, I'm uh, really flattered, Winslow. But I, I . . . can't."

His brow furrowed. "You broke up with that Seth guy, didn't you?"

"Yeah."

"Oh, I get it." His face fell. "You're already going with some-body else. I knew I should've asked —"

"That's not it," I cut in. "I just can't go with you."

His eyes sliced through me like machetes. I realized too late how that must've sounded. Before I could retract, or explain, he snarled, "I thought you were different. You're just like the rest of them." He stood, cramming his art supplies into his briefcase. Then he crashed through a row of empty chairs and wound his way to the front, to a seat as far away from me as possible.

Everyone swiveled their heads to stare at me. Especially Cece. She mouthed, What was that about?

I shot to my feet and tore out of there. God! It was all so fucked.

Chapter 23

I dove in at the deep end, driving down through the water.

Burn it off. Force it out. Make it gone.

The hiding, the secrecy, it was tearing me up inside. Why did it have to be this way? Why?

My lungs were ready to explode as I propelled off the bottom and split the surface. Then swam, lap after lap after frantic lap, trying to release it, expunge it, set it free. Set me free.

They got it wrong when they called it "the closet." This was a prison. Solitary confinement. I was locked inside, inside myself, dark and afraid and alone.

When I dragged up the stairs at Taggert House, I found Cece huddled in front of my door, a Tupperware bowl balanced on her knees. She scrambled to her feet and smiled. "Kate's special." She held the bowl out to me. "Chicken soup for the soul."

I didn't think soup was going to salve my ravaged soul. Cece shouldered her backpack and followed me inside. I dumped my crap on the floor and shoved the bowl in the microwave. Cece must've sensed my imminent implosion because she didn't ask.

The soup was comforting, or maybe it was the peace I found with Cece. We ate directly from the bowl at the dinette table. The last noodle we slurped together and kissed in the middle. Cece rinsed the bowl and spoons, then retrieved her independent living folder — the bullshit class I should've elected — kicked off her shoes, and spread out her homework on the bed.

Now her silence ragged me. I got up and headed for the closet. "Know anyone who needs a prom dress?" I wrenched out the trash bag from the back. In the bottom was the dress that Mom had ordered from a catalog. It was a seafoam green strapless number that I'd been dying to burn. Even more so now. I tossed the bag on the bed.

Cece glanced up at me, looking a little intimidated, and opened the bag. She pulled out the dress and gasped. Laying it lengthwise across the bed, she smoothed a hand down the bodice and said, "Okay, talk to me. What happened today?"

"Today, yesterday, tomorrow," I snapped. "What part of my life doesn't suck?"

Her eyes widened.

"I'm sorry," I said, calming myself. "It's just . . . everything's gone to hell."

"What do you mean?"

I told Cece about lying to Leah, the way people looked at me, the student council meeting, Seth treating me like dirt, Kirsten's confrontation in the restroom. All of it. "She called me a . . . ," my voice faltered, "a dyke."

"Ow." Cece grimaced. "Better get used to it. The best thing you can do is call yourself a dyke. A lezzie, a lesbo, a queer. All the hateful words, use them in fun. Claim them. Then they can't be used against you."

Used against me. I'd never been called names before — at least, not to my face. Never realized how much they hurt. How personal it could get. "What did I ever do to her?" I wondered aloud. "I thought Kirsten was my friend."

"Lesson number one," Cece said, "you can't always trust your friends. Lesson number two: You don't have to *do* anything to be hated for being gay."

That was the truth, I was finding out.

"But it's *their* problem, Holland." She met my eyes. "Not yours. Remember that."

Their problem. Right. So why did I feel sickened by it? Slamming the closet door, I said, "The topper, the real highlight of my day, was when Winslow asked me to the prom."

Cece's jaw dropped. "What did you say?"

"I said, 'Sure, I'd love to, Winnie. What time are you sending the limo?'"

Cece deflated visibly.

"Now he thinks I have a problem with punks, like I'm this raging bigot or something." My throat caught. "Worse than that, I hurt his feelings. Winslow Demming, the nicest guy in the world." I folded my arms around myself, aching from the memory. "It really bothers me, Cece. Not just Winslow, or Seth, or even Kirsten. All of it. Me. I'm so bound up by this secret I just want to die."

"What?" Cece breathed. "Don't say that."

"I could've done something important on the student council

this year. Promote diversity and tolerance, make a difference at Southglenn. Instead we're deciding how many fucking balloons to hang in the fucking ballroom." My fiery gaze settled on the dress, on Cece stroking it. Out of habit, I retrieved my backpack from the floor, pulled out my phone and checked it. "What does somebody 'out and proud' do about prom? Homecoming, too? All that social crap?"

"We usually go as a group," Cece said quietly. "If you want, we could go to prom together."

"Oh, right." I whirled on her. "Stand on opposite ends of the dance floor and ignore each other?" I shook my head. "I should've told her," I said, staring at the phone in my hand. "Seth, too. I should've told everyone. Not that I wouldn't have gotten the same reactions. It's just, all this fear about who knows, who's been outing me, suspecting everybody, accusing them. What difference does it make who's outing me? I should've outed myself." My eyes strayed to the window, the alley, where William was helping a new tenant-in-transition haul in boxes. "Doing this — hiding it — feels like I'm admitting it's wrong. Like I'm ashamed. I'm not ashamed. Of me or you or the way we feel about each other. I *want* the world to know." I turned back to her. "I want to be myself. I've hurt people. Leah, Winslow, Seth, my mom. Me, Ceese. *I* hurt." I pressed a hand to my heart. It felt as if the wound cut so deep it might never heal.

"Oh, God," Cece whimpered. "Why didn't you tell me?"

Why hadn't I? "Because I didn't want you to think I wasn't happy, or that I was sorry I'd fallen in love with you. I'm not. I *am* happy — with you." I couldn't hold back the truth any longer, though. "I'm afraid, Cece. I'm so alone in the world that if you

216

left me . . ." I couldn't finish the sentence, couldn't finish the thought.

"No," Cece said urgently. She scooted off the bed and came over to me. "I'm not going to leave you. What makes you think that?"

"Your lying to me. Sneaking around. Going off to Unity to be with them. The only reason I can think of that you'd lie to me is . . . there's someone else."

"No." Cece gripped my arms. "I'd *never* do that to you. Never." I wished I could believe her. I wanted to believe.

She released me and covered her face with her hands. "Oh, God." In a small voice, she said, "I have a confession to make. I lied to you. I lied to you big time."

No, please don't let her say it. Don't let her say she loves someone else.

All I could do was try to keep breathing. Keep living. Cece backed away and began to pace, rubbing her knuckles together. Nervous, jittery, the way she gets when she drinks too much coffee. As she passed me, she said, "I've betrayed you."

My heart stopped beating. Dying, dying.

"I had no right to tell you not to come out. No right. I wasn't trying to protect you. This whole keep-it-a-secret thing? It was all about me. Me." She slapped her chest. "I'm a selfish bitch."

My brain allowed her words to seep in. A selfish bitch? What did she mean? No she wasn't. Perching on the mattress, she pounded her forehead with a fist and muttered, "I ruined your life. I ruined your life by not letting you come out. I should've just stayed at Wash Central. You'd be better off if we'd never met."

"That isn't true," I said. "Stop it." She was going to injure herself if she kept battering her head. I sat beside her and pulled down her arm. "Does this have anything to do with why you transferred? What happened at Washington Central?"

She didn't answer, just sort of shrank into herself.

A long moment passed. Cece raised her head and slowly met my eyes. Nodded.

"Can you tell me?" I asked. "Please?"

She pressed her hands between her knees. "I don't want to. You'll hate me."

"I could never hate you. Please," I pleaded with her. I was so sick of all the lies and the hiding and the secrecy. Wasn't she the one who hated playing games? "Just tell me the truth, okay? I think I deserve that."

She blinked up at me and swallowed hard. "You're right. You do." She got up and padded to the closet. Easing the door back onto the runner after my slamming had dislodged it, she said, "Joanie was . . . my girlfriend. She was the first girl I ever loved. I mean, really loved. Like fireworks, you know?" She glanced over her shoulder at me.

Yeah, I knew now.

Cece added quickly, "Small fireworks compared to you."

I smiled weakly.

"But I did love her. I won't lie to you, Holland. I would've been with her forever if . . . if I could have."

I felt stung, but she was talking about the past. "Go on," I said. "What happened?"

Cece started pacing again, banging her knuckles together. "We met at this arts festival in Cherry Creek. I'd just formed

Unity and we got this invitation to do a street performance. Our first gig. Joanie was there, at the festival, working the crowd, getting signatures on a gun control petition or something. She was real active on her political action committee at school. Sort of like you and student council. That's where we met. We fell in love really fast. At least, I did." Cece found my eyes. "I'm not saying this to hurt you, Holland."

"I know. It's okay. Just tell me everything." I shoved the prom dress aside and scooted up against the headboard.

"Joanie went to a different school, St. Mary's Academy," Cece said. "Think Southglenn homophobia times ten."

I cringed. I couldn't even imagine it.

"Joanie wasn't out. Nobody was. And the last person to come out there got expelled."

"Jesus."

"Yeah, there are still places like that, believe it or not. Dark Ages. Plus, Joanie was just discovering she was gay. Sort of like you. It was the one thing we used to fight about. You can't have one person who's totally out and another who's in the closet. Well, you can, but it won't work for very long. You can't go out in public, or be with your friends —" She stopped and looked at me. "But I guess you know that."

Did I ever.

Cece plucked a pair of jeans off the floor and folded them over a kitchen chair, then stood at the window, gazing out. "In the lesbigay club at Wash Central, I was sort of in charge of helping people come out. Because there are good ways and bad ways and better times than others and things to look for in people, to gauge their attitudes and how they're going to accept you." She was talking so fast I had to listen hard to keep up. "Everybody's different," she said, turning to me and lowering herself onto the windowsill. "For some gays it's easier to tell their friends first, because the most important thing is to feel accepted by the first person you tell. And the hardest thing for most of us is coming out to our parents. But there are ways to talk to them so it's not such a shock. And you should always tell them before somebody else does." Cece averted her eyes. She got up and went to the refrigerator, opened the door and scanned the contents. Which were minimal.

Everything she'd said was swirling around in my head. I kept thinking, We should've had this conversation about coming out before. Maybe she was waiting until I was ready. Except I *was* ready. I'd been ready from the very first day.

Cece shut the fridge and turned. She smiled wistfully and said, "The best thing about coming out is, it's totally liberating. You feel like you've made this incredible discovery about yourself and you want to share it and be open and honest and not spend all your time wondering how is this person going to react, or should I be careful around this person, or what will the neighbors say?" Her eyes were sparking now, firing. "And it's more. It's about getting past that question of what's wrong with me, to knowing there's nothing wrong, that you were born this way. You're a normal person and a beautiful person and you should be proud of who you are. You deserve to live and live with dignity and show people your pride."

I welcomed the day I could be out and proud like her. Be strong and sure of myself. It's what attracted me to her in the first place. "Wow, Ceese." I hugged my knees. "I never knew about your role in the lesbigay club. How great it would be for someone who's going through this to have a person like you. Sort of a counselor, or a mentor."

Cece's face went white. She closed her eyes and squinched as if in pain. A connection — there had to be one. "Does this have something to do with Joanie?" I asked gently.

Cece fixed her gaze on the wall above my head. At my portrait of her that she'd had framed and hung over the bed. "I told Joanie all of this," Cece said. "About coming out, being out. I knew how much happier she'd be with herself if she could just break through her fear. And she understood that. She hated the hiding. But she couldn't come out at school. There was too much to lose. She was this really smart person, like you." Cece's eyes dropped to meet mine. "She had plans for college and she couldn't take the risk of being expelled. All her friends were there, too, and she didn't know how they'd deal with it. How she'd deal with it if they weren't supportive. And her parents . . ." Cece shook her head. "A lot of times we imagine these horrible things will happen when we tell them. And they usually don't."

Yeah, I thought. Then there's that time they do. I could relate to Joanie's fear.

"Over the summer, I persuaded Joanie to transfer to Wash Central where people were more accepting," Cece said. "Finally, *finally*, she decided to do it. But only after she came out to her parents."

Oh, no, I thought. Did the same thing happen to Joanie? Her parents couldn't handle it?

"I helped Joanie figure out what to say, how to break it to them. And it went better than she expected. I gave her this brochure for her parents that we keep in the lesbigay club. It sort of answers the basic questions: Is it my fault? What can I do to help? What questions should I ask my son or daughter? They were shocked, of course. But I think they already suspected. I think parents always know, they just don't want to believe it." Cece's voice changed. "They want to make it as hard on us as possible. It's such a power trip for them. Anyway," she shrugged off her rising pique, "Joanie's parents were really cool. I told her they would be. It was obvious they loved her enough."

A knife pierced my heart.

"Oh, Holland." Cece rushed to the bed and crawled across the mattress. "I'm sorry. I'm sorry. I didn't mean that about your mom. I know she loves you."

"It's okay." I fended her off with a hand. "I'm all right." Which was a lie and she knew it.

Cece's shoulders slumped and she twisted around, her back to me. "I would've advised you to do something different with your mom." She picked at the prom dress. "Maybe write her a letter. Give her time to think about it. The way your mom treated me that day, I knew she'd have a problem."

"What do you mean? How did she treat you?"

"Didn't you notice?" Cece swiveled her head. "As soon as she saw my shirt she freaked. She wouldn't even let me touch Hannah, like I was a child molester or something."

"Serious?"

Cece nodded.

I hadn't noticed. What was with my mom? Was she a flaming homophobe and I didn't even know it? "Just finish, Cece. What happened at Wash Central?"

Cece moved from the dress to fondling my ankle chain. "Joanie was like this different person after she came out to her parents. Wild and crazy and happy all the time. Because it'll do that, holding it in. It'll made you paranoid and ashamed. Not of being gay, of being such a coward. All you want to do is be honest, be the person you really are."

I know! I almost shouted. I know.

"I took it slow at first, at Wash Central. Introduced Joanie to a couple of my friends, just so she'd know what it was like being around other gay people. Because it's fantastic." She smiled over her shoulder at me. "You can talk about things that're going on in your head and in your life. You can discuss girlfriends and laugh and joke around about sex and stuff. Everybody really liked Joanie, and she liked them and it was all just hunky-dory." Cece scrambled off the bed and charged across the room. "Do we have any coffee?"

"No, we're out," I told her. "I'm sorry. I meant to stop by the store and get some after school." My mind wasn't exactly on groceries, I didn't add.

"Shit." She slammed the cabinet door over the sink.

"There's tea —"

"I hate tea. You know that."

"God."

She whirled around. Her head lolled back and she murmured, "Sorry. I'm sorry. It's just . . . this next part is hard. I never told anybody, except Mom. I didn't have to, since all my friends watched it happen." Her voice quavered.

"Come here." I opened my arms to her.

"No. Let me get through this." She took a deep breath. "So,

Joanie's like 'This is great. Why didn't I come out before? Let's tell the whole world I'm gay.' "

That sounded familiar. The irony wasn't lost on me — a lot of similarities between Joanie and me.

"I told the lesbigay club that we were going to be throwing another coming-out party. Which is what we do when a new person joins the community. So we did, and it was awesome. Joanie felt so included and accepted. And I finally had a girlfriend I could eat lunch with and bring to meetings and hold hands with in the hall. Joanie even joined Unity with me so we could be together all the time. Everybody loved Joanie and she loved everybody." Cece's eyes went black. "Especially Jenna."

Oh, my God, no. "Don't tell me."

"I am telling you," she said flatly. "She loved Jenna."

The pain in Cece's voice, in her face. "Oh, sweetheart."

Tears welled in Cece's eyes. I slid off the bed and went to her. "*I* found Joanie," she whimpered.

I hugged Cece.

"*I* loved her. She was *mine.*" Tears gushed from Cece's eyes. I'd never seen her cry. "Joanie and Jenna. How perfect," she mocked.

She must've been holding this in for months, the tears just kept coming and coming. She sobbed into my hair, gut-wrenching heaves. I hated that she was crying over Joanie. I hated more how much Joanie had hurt her.

"How can you stand having her in Unity?" I asked. "Seeing her all the time?"

Cece swiped her nose on her shirt sleeve. "I started Unity. It's my group. I'm not going to let her steal everything from me. Plus," she sniffled, "Joanie still wants to be friends. I can handle that."

Cece was strong, stronger than me. I'd kill Joanie.

Cece went into the bathroom and came out with a length of toilet paper. She blew her nose and said, "Joanie got all active in the lesbigay club, too. They elected her president and she got all these people involved in causes, like the AIDS Walk and opening our club to straights, making us a GSA. She even got asked to be on the speakers' bureau at the Center."

"God. Talk about feeling betrayed."

"No shit," Cece said. "I couldn't let you come out, Holland. Brandi was already asking about you. And my other friends, if they ever met you . . ." She paused and inhaled a ragged breath. "I couldn't let the same thing happen. You were so much like her. I said I was keeping you a secret? Yeah, I was keeping you a secret from *them*."

"Oh, Ceese."

Her eyes pooled again. "You have to hate me," she said. "Coming out is such a personal decision. You're the only one who can make it. The only one who knows when the time is right. Look what I've done to you. I've ruined your life."

"No."

"Yes! Can't you see, I'm the one who betrayed *you*. I should've let you come out. You should've told your friends. Your mom. It should've come from you. Not Seth. Not Faith. Not anyone else."

Okay, she was right about that. I guess I did feel a little betrayed, especially since Cece knew how self-destructive it was to stay in the closet. She wasn't entirely to blame, though. I'd agreed to the secret. I'd even used it as an excuse not to tell Mom. "I'm not sure it would've made a difference who told my mom," I informed Cece, smoothing her hair back from her wet cheeks.

"It might have, though." She swallowed hard. "And that's what's tearing me up inside. I made you homeless." She started to cry again.

I pressed her face between my hands. "Oh, honey. You didn't do that. My mother did. And you didn't ruin my life." I wiped the tears off her cheeks. "I'm still here, right? I should've told you how I was feeling, what was going on. We could've gotten all this out in the open earlier and talked it through. I don't hate you. I couldn't. In fact, I understand why you did it."

She blinked up at me. "You do?"

I nodded. "I'd do anything to keep you, too."

She disintegrated in tears again.

I was so relieved to finally learn the truth. Get all our feelings and fears exposed and deal with them. Cece didn't seem to share the unburdening. Even after she stopped crying, the guilt in her eyes was torturous. "You say we're alike, Ceese, but we're not," I told her. "We're different people, Joanie and me. I know *I'm* different. Why would I even look at anyone else when you're all that I've been looking for?"

"Oh, God, Holland." She crushed me in an embrace so hard, she knocked the wind out of me. It made me laugh. Made her laugh, too.

Then we couldn't stop laughing. It was wonderful, fantastic. I'd never felt such joy, freedom, and certainty. About me. About her. About us.

Trust. That's what this was about. If you can't trust the person you love, you don't have anything.

Chapter 24

Cece bought me a T-shirt. It said, NOBODY KNOWS I'M A LESBIAN. Yeah, I was coming out, but not even *I* had that much courage. Why not make an announcement over the PA? "Attention. We've just received official confirmation that Holland Jaeger is a dyke." No. I wanted to do this my way. One person at a time. Those who needed, and deserved, to be told.

I called Leah first. "I need to talk to you," I said. "If you're still talking to me, that is."

She didn't respond.

I died inside. It was too late.

"Let's meet at the clubhouse."

"The wha — oh, okay." If I could remember where it was. "When?"

"I'm too busy this week," she said.

Ow. I deserved that.

"What about Saturday?"

"Okay." I'd go crazy waiting until Saturday, but what could I do? I should be thankful she was willing to see me at all. "What time?"

"I don't know. Around four?"

"A.M.?"

"Yeah, right. Wear your pj's and bring a flashlight." She clucked her tongue. There was a smile in her voice, though.

My heart sang. "I'll be there."

"You promise this time?"

I squeezed my eyes shut. "I promise. I'll be there."

We hung up. Saturday was forever away. I couldn't put off Winslow for a whole week. I couldn't bear living with the knowledge that I'd hurt his feelings, that he basically detested me. Not when I could fix it, make it right.

Cece helped me compose a letter. I explained to Winslow how I just figured out I was gay and was trying to come to terms with it. That my saying no to him had nothing to do with him or who he was. That I really *was* flattered he'd asked me to the prom.

I signed it, "Sincerely, Holland (the turkey) Jaeger."

I was petrified to give him the letter. It didn't help that Cece had warned me, "You never know how people will react." I thought I knew Winslow, but do you ever really know a person?

The fear was immobilizing. Art period was almost over and still the letter lay under my sketchpad. Now or never. Pretending I had to sharpen my pencil, I strolled by Winslow's table up front and dropped the envelope on his pad, then skittered back to my seat.

Cece turned and met my eyes. She pressed a fist to her heart. My heart was pounding in my ears. I watched Winslow open the envelope, pull out the letter, and unfold it. He read it, then refolded it. Stared straight ahead at the white board. He didn't care. He hated me. Without warning, his chair toppled over, startling everyone. He gathered his stuff together and forged his way to the back of the room, attracting Mackel's attention with all the racket. Winslow slid into the seat beside me and said, "Yo."

It was the sweetest word I ever heard. "Yo yourself," I replied, my throat constricting. He did a really weird thing then. He looped his long arm around my shoulders and gave them a squeeze. Sort of brotherly. My eyes strayed over to Cece, who'd covered her head on the table with her arms, smothering laughter.

It was all I could do to contain my own hysteria.

▼▲▼

Paramount Park used to seem so dark and deep when we were kids. All I saw now were the weeds, the scraggly cottonwoods, the decaying litter caught in the chain-link fence. I'd completely forgotten about this place, our clubhouse.

A brilliant sun cast geometric shadows through the branches as I crunched along the overgrown trail. Trees would be budding soon, I realized. I'd always loved spring. This year's rebirth would be extra special, since it was my rebirth, too. "Knock, knock." I stood underneath our cottonwood, squinting up into the tree house.

A voice floated down, "What's the secret password?"

"Shit," I muttered.

"That's not it."

I grinned and shook my head.

"You don't remember the secret password?"

Grabbing a branch, I hoisted myself up and said, "Leah, it's been a hundred years." Another lifetime. I squeezed through the gap around the trunk, vaguely recalling there used to be a door hinged over it. "Is this floor going to hold us?" I stepped gingerly across the wobbly sheet of plywood to the far side, where Leah was sprawled against the wall of our clubhouse, reading from a spiral notebook.

"Remember this?" she asked absently.

I eased down beside her. The wood cracked and I grabbed hold of her arm to save myself — or take her with me. "What is it?" The plank held and I let her go.

Leah slid the notebook between us.

"Oh, my God. Is that our secret spy book?"

She smiled. "Remember how to read the code we invented?"

"Hell, no." It was pure hieroglyphics.

She pursed her lips at me and reclaimed the book. "Preston and Ty Mangela are stupid ugly idiots. Next time they egg us on the way home from school, we're calling the cops."

I laughed.

She continued reading, "Tiffani Enstrom is boy-crazy."

"Whoever she is." My mind wandered. Only three walls remained in our clubhouse, and two of them were in imminent danger of decay. Was it that long ago we'd discovered this place and loved it into a home? We'd strung Mom's old flowered sheets across the windows and stapled them in place. We'd even squirreled away a stash of butterscotch candies for emergencies. Where were they? In a crevice we'd chiseled out of the tree trunk.

That wasn't all we'd chiseled. I scrambled to my feet. I had to duck under a cracked limb to reach our spot. My fingers traced the letters in the bark.

"It's still here," Leah said, appearing at my side, "for all eternity, just the way we planned." She traced the carvings, too. "The history of our love lives. 'L.T. + R.R.,' " she read. "Richie Romanowski. I wonder where he is now."

"Probably in jail since he was dealing dope in sixth grade." She ignored me. " 'L.T. + D.F., L.T. + M.Z., L.T. + K.Z. . . . ' "

"You were hornier than Kirsten," I said.

She slapped my arm. "I was searching. Still am." Her eyes fixed on the tree trunk. Then slowly turned on me.

I swallowed hard. My mouth felt dry as dust. "Here's mine." I felt along the indentations. 'H.J. + . . .' "Huh." I blinked at Leah. "It's blank."

"Imagine that." Leah raised an eyebrow. "What did you want to talk to me about?"

My heart exploded in my chest. I wasn't so sure about this anymore. I thought I knew Leah, but Cece cautioned me not to expect too much. Not to be too disappointed if Leah needed some time to accept the truth. I didn't think she would . . .

I broke off a twig, then another. A knot of fear twisted my stomach.

"Do you want me to say it, or do you have like a prepared speech you've been rehearsing?"

I lowered my head and laughed to myself. Leah knew me too well. "I'm gay," I said.

She gasped and covered her mouth. But her eyes gave her away.

"You are so dead," I told her.

She grinned. Peeling off a strip of bark, she asked, "Is it Cece? Is she the one?"

My face flared. "Yeah, she's the one."

Leah meandered back to where she'd left the spiral and sat again. I followed her. "Tell me what it's like," she said.

I soared into space. These were the words I'd been longing to hear. I took a deep breath and opened myself wide. "I love her, Leah. I love her so much. I've never felt this way about anyone before. Cece and I are connected — physically, emotionally, spiritually. It's like she's inside of me." I clenched a fist to my stomach. "She's a part of me. I can't explain it. She's my soul mate."

"I hate her," Leah said.

"No." Anger gripped me. "You don't even know her."

Leah shook her head. "I don't mean that. I'm insanely jealous. I can't even imagine how it would feel for someone to love me that much."

"Oh, Leah . . ."

"I'm happy for you, Holland," she said. "But sad, too."

"Why?"

Leah ran a thumbnail down the wire spring of the notebook. "Because it changes things between us."

"No, it doesn't." I shifted to face her. "What are you talking about?"

"You're different now. You've been different. You haven't called me in months. You have a new life. New friends."

"You'll always be my friend. Always."

"But not like before. I'll never be one of you."

"One of who? God, you make it sound like a coven or something."

"Plus, you have her now. You don't need me." Unexpectedly, Leah burst into tears.

She was really bawling. This hurt her. Why? It didn't seem fair when I was so happy. I folded her in my arms and held her. Stroking her braid, I said, "You know, I used to have the worst crush on you."

If my senses hadn't been heightened, I might not have felt it. The tensing of her muscles, the slight pull away from me. I released her fast.

My brain screamed, You shouldn't have told her, you idiot! What were you thinking? I scooted back a few inches to put more distance between us.

"So, um, are you bisexual?" Leah asked, digging a tissue out of her shorts pocket. "Because . . . well, Seth and all." She blew her nose.

"No. I'm not. I realize now that I only ever loved him as a friend." By the look on Leah's face, I'm not sure she understood. I'm not sure I did, completely. "Would you do me a favor, Leah? Would you give Seth a message?"

"Sure," she said.

"Tell him I'm sorry we couldn't talk about this, that I couldn't tell him the truth. Tell him he deserves to find someone who can love him in a way I never could."

She nodded.

"You think he'll understand?"

"No," she admitted. "Not yet, anyway. He's pretty pissed. And . . . you know."

My heart ached. I never meant to hurt him. Never meant to hurt anyone. "He'll be leaving for college soon," I thought aloud. "That should help."

Leah stood up fast and walked across the plank to the other

side of the clubhouse. "Everything's changing. Everybody's leaving." Her tears threatened a rerun.

I scrabbled up after her. "You're leaving, too."

"I don't know what I'm doing. I'm definitely not going to Western State with Kirsten. She told me what she said to you." Leah met my eyes. "I couldn't believe it. Yes, I could. Kirsten's always been so jealous of you."

"Me?" I frowned. "Why?"

"Why? You're smarter than her, more popular, you have a great relationship with your mom, you have Seth. Had," she corrected herself.

"Had" was the operative word. I pressed in a loose nail on the floor. "People never see beneath the surface."

"Especially her," Leah said. "She's so shallow, all she has beneath her surface is a, a cesspool."

I widened my eyes at Leah. We both cracked up. I don't know what was so funny. The truth?

Leah shook her head. "Kirsten's such a bitch. After I let her know we were officially ex-friends, I wanted to call you so bad."

"Oh, Leah."

She added quickly, "I just wish things would stay the same forever. Don't you?"

God, no. If the cosmos hadn't shifted, if I hadn't risked change, I might never have found Cece. Found myself. I would've lived a lie, created a life around other people's expectations.

"My mom kicked me out of the house," I said.

"What?" Leah gasped. "No."

I told her everything that had transpired since Cece, deliberately leaving out the part about The Secret. That was a private

234

matter between Cece and me, our own personal history. We were building on that and it felt sort of sacred.

My eyes drifted down to my watch. "Shit. I have to go." Cece was taking me to her Unity rehearsal tonight to introduce me to her friends. It was a big step for her. For us.

Leah and I descended the tree. At the bottom, I said, "Wait. We forgot the secret spy book." I started back up.

"Leave it." She snagged my arm. "Maybe some other kids will find it and carry on the tradition." She gazed up at the crumbling clubhouse for a long moment, then looked at me. "The secret password was stewardess corp."

"What?" I made a face.

"It's an anagram for secret password."

"How lame. Who came up with that?"

"You did. I always thought it was brilliant." Leah smiled, sort of sad and nostalgic. Then she headed off through the woods.

A wave of grief washed over me. Leah would always be my friend, but she was right. Things had changed. Her world seemed very small to me, confined and limited, while mine had expanded, illuminated, grown. I saw everything now through different eyes. Wide awake and focused.

Chapter 25

There were decisions to make. My combined paychecks from Children's Cottage and Hott 'N Tott didn't begin to cover my expenses: car payment, gas, insurance, cell phone, not to mention the bare necessities like food, clothing, shelter. Taggert House shouldn't have to absorb all my living expenses, I felt. Even though Cece's uncle had hired me for the morning shift four days a week, I needed a second job that paid better. So I quit Children's Cottage. It killed me to do it, but the pay sucked, and seeing the kids every day was like this constant reminder of loss in my life.

William suggested I go down to the Center and check out their employment resources. So I did, over spring break. They hooked me up with this local moving company owned by a couple of gay guys. The work was physically demanding, but it paid well and the hours were flexible. I could work around my school schedule, plus pick up extra hours on the weekends.

Next year loomed closer on the horizon. What was I going to do with my life? Tossing a futon into a moving van wasn't exactly nuclear physics. Cece was right, I needed to think about my future. What were my options? I could work three or four jobs forever at minimum wage and scrape by. But was that all I wanted out of life, to scrape by?

There had to be more. Something was out there for me, a job, a career, a reason I was put on this earth. I hated to admit it, but maybe Mom was right. College would open a lot of doors.

Unfortunately, by the time I figured this out, it was too late to apply. At least to any colleges or universities I could afford. Plus, my grades had plummeted this semester. I'd be lucky to pull a C average.

At our Sunday gathering William broached the subject of long-range goals. He said it was important to have things to look forward to, to believe we could achieve greatness. He must've been reading my mind.

We went around the table to share what we envisioned for ourselves. I mentioned how I'd like to go to college next year, but couldn't now. William said, "Why not, hon?"

"It's too late to apply. I'll have to wait until next semester."

"You could go to Metro Urban," Ramon piped up, passing me the croissants. "That's where I go. I think you can apply up to a week before classes start."

"You're kidding. How much is tuition, since I have, like, zero money?"

"They have a gay and lesbian college fund," Ramon said. "That's how I'm doing it."

My hopes shot through the roof. "Do you have to qualify, because my grades this year suck."

Ramon shook his head. "GPA isn't all that important. They let me go cuz I beautify the campus."

William snorted. Dodging a strawberry one of the other guys threw across the table at him, Ramon added, "If you want, I could pick you up a catalog."

"No, that's okay. I can get one at school. Thanks."

I didn't dare get excited. What if they rejected me? I had nothing to fall back on — just in case.

I stalled around in the media center after school on Monday, watching the clock and waiting. When it got to feeling like a morgue, I decided now or never. The Metro catalogs would be among the state schools, stacked right outside the career center door. I could pick one up, make a run for it . . .

I turned the corner and there she was, tacking an index card onto the bulletin board. Shit.

"Um, hi, Mrs. Lucas," I faked a cheery greeting. "Can I get a Metro catalog?"

She didn't answer right away, just looked at me. Make that glared. Brrr.

"There they are." I pointed to the stack. "I'll just get one and leave."

"I don't believe you," she said.

The hair on my neck stood up. I quickly snatched a catalog.

"What about your acceptance at Stanford? Are you going to just throw that away?"

I straightened fast. "I got accepted at Stanford?"

"All the time and effort we've gone to for you, to offer you every opportunity available." She pursed her lips. "Do you know what this is doing to your mother?"

What it's doing to *her*? She's the one — Oh, forget it. I turned and stalked off. What business was it of hers? Just let me get on with my life.

I spun my combination lock and flung open the locker. My eyes were drawn to the mirror and I screamed. The person behind me jumped back a foot. "Jesus," she said, holding her heart.

"Faith?" I wheeled around. "I, uh, didn't recognize you."

She palmed her head — her shaved head. It wasn't completely bald; she'd left an inch of stubble all over the scalp. I couldn't help visualizing a hedgehog.

"I'm shedding my inhibitions," she said.

I laughed.

"No? Then how about it saves on shampoo?"

"Not even." I had the strongest urge to feel her furry head, but squelched it. Too intimate a gesture. As I loaded my backpack, Faith said, "I brought your mail." She handed me a fistful of letters. Most were bills. The letter from Stanford. The envelope had been opened, of course. Stanford was so *not* in my future. There was one letter at the bottom that made my stomach knot. Shoving the stack into my backpack, I said to Faith, "Walk me out?"

On our way to the parking lot, she asked where I was living and how I was doing. I filled her in on Taggert House, told her about my jobs. "Maybe you could come stay with us some weekend."

"Yeah?" Faith's eyebrows arched. "How 'bout this weekend? How 'bout every weekend?"

I smiled at her. "I'll ask Cece and let you know. But . . ." I hesitated. "What'll your dad say?"

"When?"

"When you tell him where you're going."

"When?"

"Faith." I widened my eyes at her.

"I'll deal with Dad. I've got him wrapped about my bloody little finger, in case you hadn't noticed. Don't worry about it."

I did worry. Felt protective. Faith needed to hold on to her family. Our family. For her, for me. While we were on the subject . . . "How is everyone?" I asked.

"About the same," she answered. "A real laugh riot. Oh, Hannah started crawling."

"Already?"

Faith nodded. "Your mom said, 'Holland oughta be here to see this.'"

My body sagged. Faith opened her mouth to say something else, but must've changed her mind. She stuck her pinkie in her mouth instead.

I evil-eyed her.

She dropped her hand.

"What?" I demanded.

She swallowed hard. "She cries. I can hear her at night."

I had to look away.

Faith added, "I just thought you should know."

I wanted to hug Faith, but couldn't. Didn't dare. Would I always have to be careful now who I touched?

Faith didn't hesitate. She threw her arms around me and drew me into her. Held me tight. How could she have known how much I needed that? I vowed to fill my life with people like Faith. People who were true to themselves.

After she left I locked myself in the Jeep. Maybe now, finally. I ripped open the envelope.

A picture fell into my lap. Hannah, in a red velvet dress, a studio shot. So cute. "Hello, Sissy." I traced her face with my index finger. "I miss you so much." Propping the picture on my dash, I unfolded the letter.

"Dear Holland," she'd written on the flowered stationery I'd given her for her birthday. "We need to talk. Why don't you call me to arrange a convenient time."

A convenient time? I lunged for my phone and started punching in numbers. I hung up before finishing the sequence. Instead, I called work and told them I'd be late.

▼▲▼

It felt weird having to ring the doorbell at my own house. In the background, I could hear the TV blaring. The whoosh of the front door startled me.

Mom stood framed in the threshold, balancing Hannah on her hip. I smiled. "Hi." She didn't move to unlock the storm door. I wondered if she was going to make me stay out on the porch, or shut the door in my face.

She twisted the latch and stepped back.

I let myself in. "I got your letter. It was sort of on my way so I didn't call first. Are you busy? Am I interrupting something? I could come back another time. Tomorrow. Or later tonight. A more convenient time." Was I babbling? Why didn't she answer? Why were her eyes tearing up?

Oh, Mom. I reached for her.

She shoved Hannah into my arms. "Would you like something to eat or drink? I need a drink."

"No, I'm fine."

241

She headed for the kitchen.

"Hannie. Hey, Sissy." I held my baby sister close and breathed her in. The fragrance of baby powder, shampoo, laundry detergent. The ginger snap all down her onesie. "God, I've missed you." I kissed her silky head.

I carried Hannah to the kitchen, where Mom was leaning over the sink, downing a tall glass of water. I wanted to open the fridge and check out the leftovers, see if there was any fried chicken. I'd been craving Mom's fried chicken.

"How are you?" she asked, wheeling around. "Your hair's getting long."

"Yeah, I'm thinking of letting it grow." Since I can't afford to get it cut, I didn't add.

"I always liked it better long." She set her glass in the sink and brushed by me, returning to the living room. I trailed with Hannah. Mom lowered herself to the sofa and remoted down the sound on the TV. I knelt on the carpet and propped Hannah in front of me, hoping she'd crawl. As if on cue, she motored across the floor like a tiny tank.

Mom and I laughed.

Good, that was good. Broke the tension.

"Where are you living?" she asked. "With that girl, I presume."

I bristled. "Her name is Cece Goddard. And no, I'm not living with Cece. I have my own place."

"How can you afford that?" Mom sniped.

Made me mad, like she knew I couldn't. Like she expected me to be living on the street, begging for handouts, bemoaning the day I disappointed her. "I manage," I said evenly.

Mom's head dropped. "I'm sorry. That was uncalled for."

My anger dissipated.

"I promised myself I'd never do to you what my parents did to me. That I'd love you no matter what. But this —" Mom raised her head and met my eyes. "I won't let you throw your life away on that girl."

A burning sensation streaked through my gut. "Her name is Cece. And what makes you think —"

"Let me finish," Mom interrupted. "You have so much talent. So much potential. I'd like to believe I had something to do with that. You can do anything you want, Holland. You have your whole life ahead of you."

"Yeah, I do," I said. "With Cece in it."

Mom exhaled irritation. She stood and hustled across the room to retrieve Hannah from the corner, where a fuzzy pacifier was finding its way into her mouth. "I don't understand this. I don't understand you. I thought you had more sense."

My insides smoldered.

Mom flipped Hannah around and headed her in the other direction. "I suppose it's some kind of phase you're going through, or an identity crisis. I don't know. It never happened to me."

"That's because you're not me. It isn't a phase."

Mom straightened. "I know you, Holland. You're not . . . that way."

Say it, I thought. Stop denying the truth. "Yes, Mother, I am. I'm gay."

"She did this to you!" Mom's voice shrilled. "I don't know what she did, but I told her mother to keep her sick daughter away from you. She's perverted, and she's preying on innocent girls —"

"You told Kate that?" Oh, my God. "How could you?" I

scrambled to my feet. I had to get over there, apologize to Kate. Oh, my God.

"Where are you going?" Mom said at my back. "Holland, I want you to come home."

That stopped me. How many times had I longed to hear those words? How many nights had I cried myself to sleep, holding the phone to my heart, praying it would ring?

"Please, listen to me," Mom's voice softened. "You don't know what you're doing, honey. You haven't thought about the consequences, what you're throwing away. Your future. Your self-respect. I'm your mother. I know you better than you know yourself."

I might've laughed. "You don't know me at all, Mom." I turned around. "All you see is this person you want me to be. And I can't be her. I'm not her. I can't live my life for you."

She spread her hands at her sides. "Please. Come home."

My eyes pooled with tears. Did I want to come home? Yes, more than anything. Not to the physical walls and floors and unlocked doors. Not to move back. But to the comfort, the security in knowing I'd always have a home. Everyone needs a home.

"And Cece?" I asked. "Is she welcome here?"

Mom's eyes slit. "She has a home."

So that's it, I thought. A parent's unconditional love — what a myth. Hannah crawled over to my feet and hoisted herself upright, clutching my leg in her strong little hands. I lifted her high into the air and captured a mental image to draw before handing her over to Mom. "Bye," I said.

"You're not getting a penny of that college money. None of it. It'll all go to Hannah." Mom snapped. "In fact, I may give it to Faith."

I shook my head at her. She didn't get it. She didn't understand at all. I loved Hannah. Faith, too. I'd be happy for them to have that money, have anything of mine.

I closed the door behind me, feeling sad for my mother. Sorry for her. Yeah, I'd made sacrifices; I'd experienced loss. But she had no idea what this was costing her. Because she was losing me.

Chapter 26

How much does it cost to rent a tux?" I asked.

Cece blinked up at me. "Are you serious?"

"I am. I think we should go to the prom."

Her eyes lit up. "I've always wanted to. I've dreamed about it."

It had been preying on my mind. I didn't know why I should have to give up my senior prom. I shouldn't have to give up everything.

I touched her face. Her gentle, golden face. "What would you wear?"

Cece bit her lip. "That green dress. It is sooo gorgeous."

I smiled. "You'd look awesome in it." She would, too.

Her expression grew serious. "But Holland, at Southglenn? I don't know. We could go as a group maybe. Safety in numbers. Brandi sort of likes this girl —"

"No," I said. "If we go, I'd want it to be just you and me. Our special night together."

Cece held my eyes for a moment, then flung her arms around my neck. "I love you," she said.

"I love you too. You and only you." I kissed her.

Our dance mix CD skipped and we both cursed. It was getting a little worn from overuse. Cece jumped off the bed to restart it.

"What is Leisure Arts?" I called to her.

"Is that a major?" She slid out the CD and put on this Norah Jones we both liked. "Sign me up."

I flipped a page in my Metro catalog. I was propped against the wall where we'd shoved Cece's bed so we'd have more floor space to dance. Since I spent so much time here lately, Kate had relaxed the house rules a bit, allowing us to hang out in Cece's room as long as the door was open. Now the battle raged over the definition of "open."

Cece sprawled backward on the bed, settling her head in my lap again. "Wow, they have an aviation technology major," I said, my fingers trailing absently through her hair. "I could learn to fly."

She slid her hand up my shirt. "I could teach you that."

I slapped her away. "You already have."

Cece grinned. Reaching up, she removed my glasses and slid them onto her face, then stuck her hands under her head, watching me. Making it extremely difficult to concentrate. I set the Metro catalog aside.

"You going to invite me to your graduation?" she asked.

"No, I'm going to make you rent the videotape."

We sneered at each other. She added, "Mom wants to know because Greg's graduating and she'd like to celebrate yours with his. Throw you both a party."

My eyebrows arched. "You're kidding."

"Would I lie to you?"

I just looked at her.

"Serious," she said. "She didn't want you to miss out on your big day."

Why did that make me feel like crying? "That's so sweet. I really love your mom. Your whole family."

Cece looped my glasses back over my ears and rolled off the bed. "I was supposed to wait to give you this, but you know me. No self-control." She dropped to her knees and scrounged under the bed. "Don't look." She straightened, twisting away. "Okay, here." She thrust a package at me. "It's from all of us. Happy graduation."

"Cece —" It was so pretty, all gold and blue. Southglenn colors.

"You'll have to wrap it back up," she said. "And act surprised. Like this." She framed her face with her hands and mimed a squeal.

It made me laugh. I slid off the satin ribbon and unwrapped the gift. It was a case. On the top was an engraved insignia of two knights on horses, jousting. "FABER-CASTELL," it read underneath. What was this, cigars? I unlatched the hook and opened the lid.

"Oh, my God," I gasped. Inside were trays of drawing supplies — pencils, chalks, pressed and natural charcoals. Dozens and dozens of watercolor pencils. "Cece, this is unbelievable." I dug out a yellow watercolor pencil and felt it come alive in my hand. What I could do with this: sunshine, roses, Cece.

"I had to promise Mom and Dad you'd draw a life-size nude of me so they could hang it over the mantel," Cece said.

I snorted.

"My own personal and extremely private present is coming later." She blew me a kiss. It made me wish later was sooner. "Oh, I have something else for you." Cece spun around and wrenched open a dresser drawer. She tossed me a T-shirt. "You can send this to your mother."

I shook it out and flipped it over. "I LOVE MY LESBIAN DAUGH-TER," it read on the front. Tears sprang to my eyes.

"Oh, no, Holland." Cece lunged at me. "It was a joke." She wound her arms around my neck. "I'm sorry. I'm sorry."

"It's okay." I peeled her off me. "It's funny. Really." I wouldn't send it, of course. Maybe one day. Cece told me to never give up hope.

She ripped the shirt out of my hands and tossed it into the closet. "I'll give it to my mom. She can add it to her collection, since I give her one every year for Christmas. Has she ever worn it? No."

"One of these days she'll surprise you," I said. "She'll have her own coming out."

"Oh, yeah. She'll be marching in the Pride Day Parade." Cece rolled her eyes.

Kate bellowed up the stairs, "What are you two doing?"

Cece hollered back, "We're doing the nasty."

"No, we're not," I volunteered. "We're just having sex." We mock-laughed at each other.

"Well, hurry it up," Kate said with a smile in her voice. "You're both going to be late for work."

"She doesn't know how late." Cece took my hand and kissed my palm.

Shiver city. "Better get changed," I said in a sigh.

Cece slipped into her work jeans and tied her bandanna on her head, while I finished the Metro Urban application. All but one question. Wow, they had a great art department. I could get a degree in graphic arts, or fine arts, or even art education. Did I want to teach? Did I even want to go into art? There was so much to choose from. Too much. And too much I didn't know about myself, too many possibilities to explore. Who knows what direction their life will take? You can't plan that.

I scanned through the list of majors again, then made my decision. Let nature take its course. On the last line I printed, "Undeclared."

Keeping You a Secret

A Letter from Julie Anne Peters

Dear Readers,

When it was suggested to me that I write a lesbian love story, I thought it was a crazy idea. I'd be coming out of the closet all over again—this time on a global scale. I'd be putting both myself and my partner at risk. I'd get hate mail. Besides, who would read this book?

The last question was answered in volumes. When *Keeping You a Secret* was first published, my e-mail box began to fill with hundreds and hundreds of letters. Young readers wrote to tell me how much they loved the book and how closely it paralleled their lives. They shared their own coming-out stories, their fears, uncertainties, trials, and triumphs. Like Holland and Cece in the book, more than anything young people wanted love, to have their love validated and recognized as real.

There were readers who seemed happy and well-adjusted. But I also heard from too many young people who were in such despair about being gay that they'd tried to hurt themselves. These letters did, and still do, make me cry. I received mail from straight kids who identified with the ostracism and harassment issues in the book. Older readers wrote and thanked me for the book and expressed their regret at not having this kind of literature available to them when they were growing up.

Clearly, there is an eager, hungry audience yearning for contemporary literature that depicts their lives, exposes the myths, reveals the truth, and illuminates the contributions of LGBTQ (Lesbian, Gay, Bisexual, Transgender, Questioning) people to home, family, and society.

There was no hate mail. A few disparaging comments that momentarily shook my faith. But then a letter would arrive from a young reader – twelve or fourteen or sixteen – who'd say, "I love this book so much. You don't know what you've done for me."

Readers, from my heart to yours: May you find the happiness you seek, the peace and joy and comfort of community. May you be safe and secure and strong. Be proud of who you are. Be visible so you can see each other, find each other, show the world our humanity. Be true to yourself and those you love. Use the words and actions against you to strengthen your will. Teach acceptance and celebration of difference and diversity. Keep your sense of humor. Recognize your place in history and continue to work for positive, peaceful social change.

Your letters remind me that I need to take my own advice. Many thanks to you, readers and writers, for your kindness, trust and encouragement.

There is no sequel planned for *Keeping You a Secret*. But I do intend to write many more books for and about us, books I hope will resonate and rejoice in our lives.

Love,

Julie

Keeping You a Secret

Questions for Discussion

1. What expectations are placed on you by your parents as a son or daughter? Do you feel expectations as a student? As a friend? Girlfriend or boyfriend? Do you expect things of yourself? Are expectations good or bad? Do expectations shape your life?

2. A recurring theme in *Keeping You a Secret* is honesty—telling the truth about yourself, to yourself and to others. Can you think of a time in your life when you didn't acknowledge the truth about yourself? Why did you hold back?

3. Give specific examples where the story and setting in *Keeping You a Secret* reflect current social and political attitudes. Do you find the same attitudes exist where you live? Why do you think there are regional differences in the level of discrimination and tolerance?

4. What stereotypes exist about lesbians and gays? Where do stereotypes come from? Do you ever feel you're stereotyped and judged?

5. What obstacles did Holland have to overcome to get to the truth that she was a lesbian? Why do you think it took Holland so long to come to terms with it?

6. Coming out is a difficult, personal process. What do you think makes it so hard for most people? If you're going through the coming-out process, describe your experiences, both positive and negative.

7. Do you think the culture at your school or work contributes to a climate of fear among lesbian and gay people? How? What can be done about that? Are you responsible? Who is?

8. Does your school have a Gay/Straight Alliance? Would you join if it did?

9. If you found out your best friend was lesbian or gay, how would you react? What if it was your sister or brother? Your mother or father? Would it change the way you feel about them? Would it change the way you feel about yourself?

10. Do you think being gay is a choice? As a lesbian or gay person, are there choices to be made in the way you live your life? How can you empower yourself? Do you feel you can change your nature? Would you want to?